THE FACE C

JOHN BLACKBURN was born in 1923 in the village of Corbridge, England, the second son of a clergyman. Blackburn attended Haileybury College near London beginning in 1937, but his education was interrupted by the onset of World War II; the shadow of the war, and that of Nazi Germany, would later play a role in many of his works. He served as a radio officer during the war in the Mercantile Marine from 1942 to 1945, and resumed his education afterwards at Durham University, earning his bachelor's degree in 1949. Blackburn taught for several years after that, first in London and then in Berlin, and married Joan Mary Clift in 1950. Returning to London in 1952, he took over the management of Red Lion Books.

It was there that Blackburn began writing, and the immediate success in 1958 of his first novel, *A Scent of New-Mown Hay*, led him to take up a career as a writer full time. He and his wife also maintained an antiquarian bookstore, a secondary career that would inform some of Blackburn's work, including the bibliomystery *Blue Octavo* (1963). *A Scent of New-Mown Hay* typified the approach that would come to characterize Blackburn's twenty-eight novels, which defied easy categorization in their unique and compelling mixture of the genres of science fiction, horror, mystery, and thriller. Many of Blackburn's best novels came in the late 1960s and early 1970s, with a string of successes that included the classics *A Ring of Roses* (1965), *Children of the Night* (1966), *Nothing but the Night* (1968; adapted for a 1973 film starring Christopher Lee and Peter Cushing), *Devil Daddy* (1972) and *Our Lady of Pain* (1974). Somewhat unusually for a popular horror writer, Blackburn's novels were not only successful with the reading public but also won widespread critical acclaim: the *Times Literary Supplement* declared him 'today's master of horror' and compared him with the Grimm Brothers, while the *Penguin Encyclopedia of Horror and the Supernatural* regarded him as 'certainly the best British novelist in his field' and the *St James Guide to Crime & Mystery Writers* called him 'one of England's best practicing novelists in the tradition of the thriller novel'.

By the time Blackburn published his final novel in 1985, much of his work was already out of print, an inexplicable neglect that continued until Valancourt began republishing his novels in 2013. John Blackburn died in 1993.

# THE FACE OF
# THE LION

## JOHN BLACKBURN

*With a new introduction by*
**GREG GBUR**

**VALANCOURT BOOKS**

*The Face of the Lion* by John Blackburn
First published London: Jonathan Cape, 1976
First Valancourt Books edition 2013

Published by Valancourt Books, Kansas City, Missouri
*Publisher & Editor*: JAMES D. JENKINS
*20th Century Series Editor*: SIMON STERN, University of Toronto
http://www.valancourtbooks.com

*Library of Congress Cataloging-in-Publication Data*

Blackburn, John, 1923-
  The face of the lion / John Blackburn ; with a new introduction
by Greg Gbur. – First Valancourt Books edition.
    pages ; cm. – (20th century series)
  ISBN 978-1-939140-43-2 *(acid free paper)*
  I. Title.
  PR6052.L34F33 2013
  823'.914–dc23

                                    2013009350

# INTRODUCTION

THE word 'zombie' appears nowhere in John Blackburn's 1976
horror novel *The Face of the Lion*, but it is nevertheless very much
a novel about zombies. Furthermore, it is perhaps one of the
earliest novels to explore the implications of a contagious plague
of zombie-like creatures, though the author would not pursue the
idea to its most apocalyptic consequences. Even so, *The Face of the
Lion* is a well-crafted mixture of horror, thriller and mystery of a
style unique to Blackburn that irresistibly pulls the reader along.

If John Blackburn (1923-1993) had missed out on an opportunity
to be at the vanguard of what is now a cultural phenomenon, his
career did not suffer for it. By the time *The Face of the Lion* was
published in 1976, he had been a successful author for nearly two
decades, a career that began with the immediately successful *A
Scent of New-Mown Hay* in 1958 and eventually ended with his 28th
novel *The Bad Penny* in 1985. His novels were generally well received
by critics, and in retrospect he is considered 'an important figure in
British horror fiction in particular, a transitional figure between the
older style of weird fiction practiced by Dennis Wheatley and the
later type of horror written by the popular author James Herbert.'[1]

Before settling on a career as an author, Blackburn performed
a variety of jobs, working earlier in life as a lorry driver, then later
as a schoolmaster in London and then a teacher in Berlin. During
World War II, he served as a radio officer in the Mercantile Marine.
In 1952 he settled into a position as the director of Red Lion Books
in London, and it was there that he began to work on his first
books. With the success of the first two in 1958, he quit to pursue
writing full time. Though he left the publishing world, he did run
an antiquarian bookstore with his wife, a pursuit that would play
an important role in some of his works.

1 From John Blackburn's entry in the *Dictionary of Literary Biography*, DLB 261,
pp. 98-102.

Blackburn's fiction is an unpredictable mix of mystery, thriller, horror, espionage, and even at times science fiction. His oeuvre is roughly split evenly between stories with a horror focus and more conventional spy/mystery tales. However, even the latter typically have a gruesome revelation in them. Blackburn was a master of mystery, and would introduce numerous red herrings and plot twists to keep the reader guessing until the very end. His stories are fast-paced and generally convey the impression of a series of increasingly dire events spiraling out of control.

The Face of the Lion is a typical example of Blackburn's style of thriller, if 'typical' is an appropriate word to describe any of his work. The novel begins, as many of his do, with a number of violent murders. A woman visiting her grandmother's house in a remote area of Scotland meets an awful fate when she comes face to face with an intruder in the house; not far away, an agent for British Intelligence is gunned down while investigating a region of the countryside that has been cordoned off for unknown reasons by local lord and hero Sir James Fraser Clyde. Clyde, a wealthy landowner and businessman, is a staunch and vocal advocate for Scottish independence from the United Kingdom. When news reaches British Intelligence that Clyde has posted armed guards outside an area surrounding his mining operation, officials fear that he is working on a nuclear weapon. However, the truth is far worse than they could imagine: Clyde's men are trying to contain an unknown contagion that turns those it infects into swollen, rampaging beasts – beasts that can infect others with a touch. Soon Colonel Lawrence of the Internal Security Service and bacteriologist Marcus Levin find themselves racing to contain the plague and find its origin before it is unleashed upon the entire country.

The similarities of The Face of the Lion to modern stories of the zombie apocalypse should be quite clear even from the short description above. Blackburn's monsters are not, of course, the traditional 'living dead'. As we have noted, the word 'zombie' does not appear in the novel at all – though to be fair, it also does not appear in George Romero's classic Night of the Living Dead, to be discussed below. The Face of the Lion fits into a bigger collection of tales that began with the living dead and have grown to encompass a large number of 'zombie-esque' creatures. These creatures all share a number of characteristics: the loss of humanity, hatred of the uninfected, and the ability to spread their contagion through a bite or a scratch.

To put Blackburn's novel in its proper context, it is worthwhile to look briefly at the history of zombies in fiction. This is no simple task – the evolution of the zombie story is quite complex and spans well over a hundred years and includes countless books and movies. Nevertheless, even an abridged history can give insight into Blackburn's take on the genre.

The apocalyptic zombie stories of today developed from the merging of two originally disparate story genres. The most obvious is the adoption of Haitian voodoo legends into movies and stories about the walking dead. Much earlier than this, however, were so-called 'last man' stories, involving the near-extinction of humanity by an apocalyptic plague or other catastrophic event.

The earliest of these is the 1805 novel *Le Dernier Homme* (*The Last Man*) by Jean-Baptiste François Xavier Cousin de Grainville. It is a religious tale that describes a future in which humanity's ability to reproduce has faltered, and the coming of the Biblical apocalypse will be determined by the fate of the last man and woman on earth. Not long after, a much less spiritual catastrophe titled *The Last Man* was penned in 1826 by none other than Mary Shelley. Though the bulk of the novel is a rather sentimental tribute to Shelley's departed friends, a terrible plague strikes in the latter half, leaving a sole survivor to reminisce about loneliness and mankind's lost glory. Many other works with a similar theme followed, such as M.P. Shiel's 1901 novel *The Purple Cloud*, which describes an arctic expedition that precipitates the death of every air-breathing creature on earth – save one.

Of all these early works, the literary movement towards a zombie apocalypse is most clear in H.G. Wells's 1933 novel *The Shape of Things to Come*. Wells describes a 1956 worldwide pandemic of 'maculated fever' that occurs in the aftermath of a world war. The description of the sufferers should seem familiar to zombie fiction aficionados:

One terror which is never omitted is the wandering of the infected. Nothing would induce them to remain in bed or hospital; nothing could keep them from entering towns and houses that were as yet immune. Thousands of these dying wanderers were shot by terror-stricken people whom they approached [. . .] For awhile, under such desperate and revealing stresses, man ceased to obey the impulses of a social animal. Those of the population who resisted the infection – and with maculated fever the alternatives were immunity or death – gave way to a sort of despair and hatred against the filthy suffering around them. Only a few men with medical, military, priestly or police training seem to have made head against the disaster and tried to maintain a sort of order. Many plundered. On the whole, so far as the evidence can be sifted, women behaved better than men, but some few women who joined the looters were terrible.

Sufferers of the 'wandering sickness'[1] are already remarkably close to modern zombies, though they lack the aggression and hunger for human flesh. At about the same time, however, the 'walking dead' were beginning to shamble their way into the public imagination, and would merge spectacularly with the 'last man' to produce a cultural phenomenon.

Voodoo first made a big impression on the public thanks to the writings of Hesketh Hesketh-Pritchard,[2] who traveled across Haiti in 1899 for a magazine assignment. His writings were collected in the 1900 book *Where Black Rules White, A Journey Across and About Hayti*, and gave lurid accounts of the ability of 'Vaudoux' practitioners to poison people and take them into and out of a deathlike trance:

There is another operation to which the Papalois – or more often the Mamalois – turn their power. They can produce a sleep which is death's twin brother. For instance, a child marked for the Vaudoux sacrifice is given a certain drug, shivers and in some hours sinks into a stillness beyond the stillness of sleep. It is buried in

1 The disease is called the 'wandering sickness' in the 1936 film adaptation of Wells's novel, titled *Things to Come*.

2 Hesketh-Pritchard is also known for writing, with his mother, the 'Flaxman Low' stories about a psychic detective, some of the first of their kind.

due course, and later, by the orders of the Papalois, is dug up and brought to consciousness; of what occurs then I have written in another place.

The idea of using chemicals and/or supernatural powers to control people was immediately seized by writers of the macabre; in Richard Marsh's 1905 novel *A Spoiler of Men* (also published by Valancourt Books), an unscrupulous chemist makes slaves of his unwitting victims. The 'zombi' itself was popularized by explorer William Seabrook's own 1929 account of Haitian practices, *The Magic Island*. This book inspired the first zombie movie, *White Zombie* (1932), a macabre love story in which a jilted man turns the object of his affection into one of the undead.

With both apocalyptic and undead elements in the public consciousness, it was perhaps only a matter of time before they were joined together. This was done spectacularly in Richard Matheson's novel *I Am Legend*, published in 1954 (not far off from the date of Wells's predicted apocalypse). In the book, sole survivor of humanity Robert Neville fights to stay alive in a world in which all other humans have been turned into vampire-like creatures, hungry for Neville's blood. Though the creatures are vampires, not zombies, the story has all the elements of a modern apocalyptic tale. Matheson's work would then inspire an even more influential horror story: George Romero's 1968 movie *Night of the Living Dead*, in which the dead awaken due to the radiation from an exploded space probe, and hunt humans en masse.

Romero's film stunned and appalled audiences. As film critic Roger Ebert noted in his original review:[1]

> The kids in the audience were stunned. There was almost complete silence. The movie had stopped being delightfully scary about halfway through, and had become unexpectedly terrifying. There was a little girl across the aisle from me, maybe nine years old, who was sitting very still in her seat and crying.
>
> I don't think the younger kids really knew what hit them. They

---

1 Taken from rogerebert.com. I suspect there is a typo on the page, however, which dates the review January 5, 1967; the film premiered on October 1, 1968!

were used to going to movies, sure, and they'd seen some horror movies before, sure, but this was something else.

*Night of the Living Dead* sparked countless imitators, starting with a collection of low-budget films in the 1970s by Italian, American, and British filmmakers. At the same time, George Romero filmed a different take of 'horror in mass numbers' in the 1973 movie *The Crazies*, about a town that is accidentally exposed to a biological weapon that turns its occupants insane. It was in this atmosphere that John Blackburn's 1976 *The Face of the Lion* was written. Blackburn's book contains most of the elements of zombie horror that are now familiar, including the spread of contagion through bite or scratch, desperate attempts to quarantine the outbreak, and the creation of the disease through reckless scientific experimentation. Blackburn's zombies are not the slow lumbering beasts of Romero's movie, however; they are fast moving savage hulks. In this, Blackburn seems to have anticipated the 'fast zombie' craze of recent years, as they appear in movies such as *28 Days Later* (2002), the remake of *Dawn of the Dead* (2004) and the horror comedy *Zombieland* (2009).

There is no clear evidence that Blackburn was inspired by *Night of the Living Dead*; the author stayed out of the public eye and did not talk much about the genesis of his stories. However, a survey of his work indicates that he liked to take advantage of current popular trends in horror. His 1959 novel *Broken Boy*, for instance, is similar to the popular stories of Satanism written by Dennis Wheatley years earlier; also, his novel *Nothing but the Night* (1968) seems to be inspired by the spate of 'evil children' stories that were popular at the time. In each case, however, Blackburn struck out in new directions, taking the original concept and pushing it to new and darker places.

It is even fair to say that Blackburn anticipated *Night of the Living Dead* in his earlier writings. Many of the author's books are based on the race to stop a new and deadly strain of disease; this includes his very first novel *A Scent of New-Mown Hay* (1958). The disease in this novel even turns its victims into mutated rampaging monsters, though the monsters are a far cry from the living dead. Other

Blackburn novels with disease-themed plots include *A Ring of Roses* (1965), *The Young Man from Lima* (1970) and *Devil Daddy* (1972).

This reliance on similar plot devices may have worked against Blackburn by the time *The Face of the Lion* was published; the book was received less favorably than his earlier work. A review that appeared in the *Winnipeg Free Press* on April 24, 1976 said, 'As a horror story this wouldn't curdle week old milk in a thunderstorm.' Maurice Richardson, writing in *The Observer* on February 29, 1976 commented, 'If I were his publisher I'd advise sedation.' However, the March 4, 1976 review in *The Guardian* by Matthew Coady says the novel '[k]eeps absurdity at arm's length and achieves a delicious sense of nausea.'

The negative critics might have revised their opinions if they could see how potent the zombie idea would become, and how ahead of the game Blackburn was in writing about it. Printed fiction about the zombie apocalypse was relatively rare through the 1980s and 1990s, with the notable exception being the 1989 *Book of the Dead*, edited by John Skipp and Craig Spector, an anthology of stories by some of the best horror authors of the day which was inspired by Romero's apocalyptic work. Soon after the turn of the millennium, however, authors began to produce powerful stories about the living dead (in some form) running rampant. Books such as Brian Keene's 2003 *The Rising*, Stephen King's 2006 *Cell* and Max Brooks's 2006 *World War Z* helped revitalize the zombie genre, which is now a cultural phenomenon that seems likely to persist. Even Blackburn's vision of a world of people driven into mad rage has been echoed by later books such as Jim Starlin and Daina Graziunas's *Among Madmen* (1990) and Simon Clark's *Blood Crazy* (1995).

So what are zombie apocalypse stories really about, and why have they become so popular? I suspect that there is no simple answer to the first question: zombie stories can be used to convey a variety of ideas and prey upon a variety of fears. Apocalypse stories in general are often about loneliness, even in the heart of society. Zombie plagues can represent our worst fears about disease and infection. George Romero, in his 1978 *Dawn of the Dead*, used zombies to mock America's brain-dead consumerism.

Zombie apocalypse tales can be used as a setting to test the limits of human compassion and endurance. This plethora of ideas that can be conveyed with the living dead run amok is likely why such stories are popular: dead men can be used to tell quite a lot of tales.

GREG GBUR
*March 23, 2013*

Special thanks to author Brian Keene for a helpful discussion of zombie apocalypse history. If there are any mistakes in this introduction, however, they are mine alone.

GREG GBUR is an associate professor of physics and optical science at the University of North Carolina at Charlotte. He writes the long-running blog 'Skulls in the Stars', which discusses classic horror fiction, physics and the history of science, as well as the curious intersections between the three topics. His science writing has recently been featured in 'The Best Science Writing Online 2012,' published by Scientific American. He has previous introduced John Blackburn's *Broken Boy*, *Nothing but the Night*, and *Bury Him Darkly* for Valancourt Books.

# THE FACE OF THE LION

# One

' "English greed and Scottish shame . . . Charlie's spirit burns again . . ." ' Mary Alison sang loudly and tunefully while she free-wheeled down the lane with Buster, the family's cross-bred sheepdog, gambolling in front of her bicycle. ' "Jaimie will relieve our pain, and we shall be free." '

If Mary's father had caught her singing that particular ballad he'd have taken his strap to her without hesitation. A patriotic Scot, Colin Alison, but a man of peace and a kirk elder who abominated racial hatred and thoroughly distrusted the song's hero.

' " . . . and we shall be free." ' To hell with Dad, Mary thought, repeating the line. Dad couldn't hear her and she was going to see Grandma. Dear, wise old Gran who believed in the laird's crusade and had often shaken the hand of the great man himself. The hand of Sir James Alistair Fraser Clyde, who could trace his descent from Bonnie Prince Charlie, Scotland's last true king. Jaimie Clyde, the Smilin' Boy, who hated the money-grubbing English and was going to release the country from their yoke.

Such a lovely country, too. Mary looked at the vistas spread out around her. To the right lay the Atlantic, with two tugs bobbing on the swell; the *Cana* and the *Galtee Girl*, searching for the wreck of an Armada treasure galleon which had foundered off Nevern Head. Up to the present the boats had found nothing, but they would in time. Everything Jaimie Clyde did was bound to succeed: only last week a coffin containing the body of the Spanish captain had been recovered from a marsh called the Field of Ugliness. That proved the wreck existed, and soon the tugs would raise the treasure and the people would be rich.

And there was another source of wealth in the area. Mary looked at the hills dominating the peninsula: gentle, heather-covered slopes rising to the scree shoots, scree solidifying into precipices, and towering above them all the vast, jagged ridges of Ben Sagur. The Hollow Mountain, as it had been nicknamed since the mining operations started – the biggest mountain in the neighbourhood. A mountain that contained enormous deposits of gold.

'God bless and keep you, Sir James Clyde.' At thirteen, Mary was already an impassioned disciple of the laird and she muttered the prayer fervently. Clyde and his men were up in those hills now, carrying out military exercises to prepare themselves in case there was interference from the authorities, and Mary's heart was with their leader. The laird was her hero. A demi-god who laughed at danger, and though the politicians in Edinburgh and London disapproved of his plans, what did the Smilin' Boy care? No one would dare to lay a finger on him. Gran had said that even the Prime Minister was frightened of Jaimie Clyde – and what harm did Jaimie do? He did nothing but good. The miners and the tug-boat crews had been out of work before the schemes started and the foreigners he'd brought in were decent, respectable folk. Why should they be interfered with?

Such a lovely country; such a lovely day. The downward slope ended where the lane crossed a stream and from then on the route to Gran's cottage ran uphill. The air was warm, the water beneath the bridge was tempting and Buster, who had already taken a dip, was shaking himself dry on the bank.

A lovely day – just the day for a bathe. Mary started to brake and then she recalled a quotation from a history book. 'What a lovely day to die on.' That was what Marie Antoinette, the French queen, had said when they took her to the guillotine. There was no time to go swimming; Gran was sick and she needed the medicine.

'Only a mild touch of flu, but she'd better have an antibiotic,' Dr Mackenzie had told Mary's mother. 'Have the lass collect this prescription from the chemist and get it over to her as soon as possible.' That was the reason for Mary's visit, so she resisted the tempting water and pedalled on.

Her grandmother's house stood on the lower slopes of Ben Sagur and was far away from any other building. A single-storeyed, whitewashed cottage surrounded by tiny, stone-walled fields. The lane leading to it steepened sharply towards the end of the journey and Mary was panting before she finally dismounted and pushed the bicycle up the last few hundred yards. But the smoke rising from the chimney was like a flag raised in welcome and the thought of seeing dear old Gran made her shrug aside exhaustion. She felt waves of happiness come over her as she reached the garden gate and leaned the cycle against a wall. She took a tube of tablets from its saddlebag and paused.

'Go on, Buster. What's the matter with you, boy?' She frowned in surprise, because the dog usually bounded to the door and barked for admission. But now he was hanging back with tail drooping and hackles up, and Mary's happiness turned to anxiety. Did animals sometimes sense disaster? Did Buster's behaviour mean that Gran was really ill – that her life was in danger?

Of course not. Buster was a fool and a mild touch of flu was what Dr Mackenzie had said. Surely people – even old people – didn't die of that? Mary reassured herself as she ran to the front door which was never locked, just as Gran's fire was never allowed to go out. She opened the door with a shout of greeting and then stopped in her tracks, her heart pounding and her breath coming in gasps.

'Gran – Gran – for the love of God, Gran.' Her grandmother might be old, but she was a meticulous housekeeper. 'A place for everything and everything in its place,' was one of her favourite maxims, and whenever Mary had visited the cottage it had been in apple-pie order. Not on this visit, however, and she stared in horror at the ruin confronting her.

The living-room was a shambles. The big, bow-fronted cabinet, which was Gran's pride and joy, lay face down on the floor with broken glass and crockery littered around it. The covers of the chairs and the horsehair sofa had been slashed. A bowl of waxed fruits, another of Gran's treasures, was broken and its contents strewn on the hearth-rug. Long-preserved apples and oranges and pears gleamed in the sunlight which sparkled through the window-panes.

Worst of all in Mary's eyes was the fate of Reddie and Rusty, the two stuffed squirrels she had played with when she was a baby. Somebody had tossed them into the fire and the little bodies were smouldering on the peat.

'Who did this, Gran? Where are you, Gran?' The bedroom door

had been torn from its hinges and Mary saw more evidence of
vandalism. The bed and the dressing-table and the washstand were
overturned, and a plaster crucifix had been pulled from the wall
and trampled into fragments.

Who was responsible? Burglars? Gipsies? Maniacs? Or bloody
English tourists? Several possible culprits flickered through Mary's
dazed mind, but the last seemed the most feasible. Drunken louts
who called themselves hill-walkers and enjoyed destroying things.
Not so long ago, a gang of them had camped on Farmer Angus's
land without permission and set fire to a barn when he ordered
them off. Hooligans who'd think it was funny to persecute an old,
sick woman.

Certainly not burglars. Thieves don't destroy valuable possessions; they steal them. And not gipsies or tourists either. Since the
Angus business Jaimie Clyde had forbidden strangers to camp in
the area. A maniac must have ransacked the house – a madman
who might have killed Gran too. Mary Alison was only a young,
frightened child; she couldn't imagine any other solution, but she
was soon to discover one.

'Oh, Gran. Where are you, Gran?' she whimpered, and then
broke off abruptly, realizing she was not alone. The kitchen door
was closed and from behind it came a sound. A grunting, guzzling,
slobbering sound which reminded her of pigs jostling around a
swill tub. A sound that made her forget about Gran and think of
her own safety, though she couldn't run away. Tears were blinding her, her feet seemed to be nailed to the floorboards, the pills
dropped from her hand.

Outside in the garden the dog whined twice and then bolted off
down the hill. Inside the cottage the sound increased. The kitchen
door opened.

## Two

'Infuriating for you, Jock, most annoying. So let's have another
round on the house.' Michael Mileham, proprietor of the Red
Deer Hotel at Frasermuir, sometimes remarked that he lived by

THE FACE OF THE LION 7

his nose, which was long and thin and curved like a hawk's beak. The implication was that he used the organ to test the quality of his food and drink, but that was only partly true. The Red Deer was a small establishment and Mickey Mileham had a more absorbing interest. He was a smeller of news.

'A large Teacher's for Mr Andrews, lass, and a couple of jars for Jock and Alec. No, on second thoughts, nothing for me.' Mileham laid a hand over his empty glass and grinned at the three men seated beside him at the table. Sergeant Andrews of the local police, Jock Stuart, a farmer, and a traveller in animal-feeds named Alec Richardson. 'I have a date with his lordship's grouse this afternoon and must keep my wits about me.

'A bit strange that your chaps weren't informed in advance, Sergeant. High-handed, one might almost say.'

'Just an oversight, Mr Mileham.' The policeman added a dash of water to his whisky. 'The laird will know about it right enough and he's the man who matters; Chief Constable, Fiscal, and High Sheriff.'

'Also our principal landowner and chairman of the Coronsay Development Corporation.' Mileham glanced at a coloured photograph of the laird on the wall. Sir James Fraser Clyde wore full Highland dress, and his face under the blue bonnet and eagle's feather was a handsome one. An intelligent face too, though there was something wrong with the eyes. They were set very close together and didn't seem to focus quite correctly.

'You say that blasting was the foreman's explanation, Jock?' While he spoke Mileham considered the information he had already received. 'A pretty lame excuse, because the road runs nowhere near the mining site. No reason to stop law-abiding citizens going about their daily business, Sergeant. Jock should have been away in the hills buying cattle and Alec had an appointment in Liskerg this morning. However much we respect the laird, his people are rather a law to themselves.'

'Ah, forget it, Mickey.' The door had opened and Alec Richardson became guarded as he recognized the man entering the room. A well-mannered man who bowed politely to the company though he didn't smile, and Mileham knew why. Plastic surgeons had done a wonderful job on him, but his facial muscles were beyond repair. Mileham also knew what had caused the injuries. His guest was an ex-I.R.A. Provisional and one of his own bombs had exploded a trifle too soon.

'My business wasn't all that pressing. Anyway, what does an extra half hour on the road matter?' Richardson was beginning to regret mentioning the incident, though it had made him angry at the time. The detour sign which he'd ignored until men – men with shotguns and sporting rifles – had flagged him down. The quarry foreman who had ordered him to turn the car round and go a good fifteen miles out of his way. Very annoying, but in that part of Scotland it was unwise to criticize Sir James Clyde and the Development Corporation. 'Let's change the subject, for Christ's sake.'

'You're right, Alec. Dead right, and of course the foreman's explanation was correct. They're going to start blasting near the road junction and someone forgot to notify the police.' Mileham eased back his chair knowing that he would receive no more enlightenment. The man quietly sipping a dry sherry at the bar worked for Clyde and his presence was as effective as a physical gag.

All the same, the news was disturbing. The laird appeared to have sealed off the entire Ben Sagur peninsula and posted armed guards at the road blocks. Nothing really odd about that perhaps. Sir James Fraser Clyde was an autocrat and a visionary with dreams of salvaging a treasure galleon and finding gold in a mountain. But Clyde had other dreams, and, coupled with information Mileham had learned earlier, something extremely sinister could be in the offing.

And when one considered the terrain . . . Mileham looked at a panoramic view of Ben Sagur above the bar and he realized that he would have to make a personal investigation. 'Will you excuse me, gentlemen,' he said, standing up and smiling at Stuart and Richardson and the policeman. 'I've enjoyed our chat, but I must keep my date with them wee birds.'

Mickey Mileham nodded to the barmaid and the quiet man at the counter and strode out of the room. He did have an appointment, but not with birds.

He was about to meet the Last Enemy.

The direct route to Liskerg followed the coast road for six miles and then crossed the base of the Ben Sagur peninsula and headed north-east. A rough, narrow road that twisted and spiralled to avoid the rocky outcrops which heralded the mountains looming up on three horizons.

But, in spite of the bends and the uneven surface, Mileham made good progress. News of the detour had got around; most travellers were taking the longer inland route and traffic was almost non-existent. The speedometer of his Land Rover rarely fell below 40 miles an hour, and while he drove he considered his mission and his master.

Mickey Mileham had bought the Red Deer six months after retiring from the Service, and he'd run it for over two years before Colonel Lawrence paid him a visit. Not a long period of time, but he hadn't recognized Lawrence at first. The colonel, formerly a slim, upright man, had aged prematurely. His back was bent, his red hair was flecked with grey and he had a decided paunch. But after signing the visitors' register and saying he'd come up for the trout season, some of his old hearty manner had returned and he expanded his statement. Mileham had a nose for news as well as food and drink, and Bill Lawrence was an angler – a fisher of men.

'Well, Mickey,' he'd asked when they were alone in the residents' lounge. 'What do you think of that fellow? What's he up to? What makes him tick?'

'I can't speak for his character, Colonel, but he's done a lot of good for the district.' Mileham followed Lawrence's stare at another photograph of James Fraser Clyde. It was policy to display the laird's picture in every public room. 'You could describe him as a despot, I suppose. Virtually a feudal overlord, though a benevolent one apparently. Most of the people worship him, because he's given them work and a sense of national dignity.'

'National dignity!' Lawrence snorted over his brandy. 'Two contemptible words which are responsible for half humanity's troubles.

'And as for *work*,' he made that word sound equally contemptible,

'Clyde is squandering a vast fortune on completely unprofitable projects. I suppose that Ben Sagur might contain enough gold to make a few dozen wedding-rings, but historians have proved that the *Santa Veronica* galleon had no treasure on board. Wild-goose chases, Mickey, or maybe something else. Smoke-screens to hide another project which is being directed by highly-paid outsiders. Some of them foreign exiles who probably entered this country under false names and forged passports.' Lawrence had paused to light a cigarette, and there was an expression in his eyes that Mileham recognized. The colonel was worried.

'I've come to you for help, Mickey, and you're in an excellent position to give it.' His next statement confirmed Mileham's suspicions. 'As the proprietor of a public house you must hear a lot of loose talk, so are you prepared to return to harness? Will you try to find out what the Smilin' Boy, as they call him, is really up to?'

'Yes, sir.' Mileham made up his mind immediately and after one week he hadn't regretted the decision. The laird was after more than Armada treasure and mountain gold, and he was not merely an autocrat. He had a private fighting force of gillies and tenants, and as he was High Sheriff the police turned a blind eye on their activities. He also had his foreign technicians and Mileham was certain Lawrence had been right about their false identities. Secretive persons who didn't talk about their pasts. Talented persons with scientific knowledge.

How deserted the road was, he thought as the miles slid by. It was market day in Liskerg. Normally the coast road would have been busy, but he had only seen two vehicles since leaving Frasermuir. News of the restriction must have spread like wildfire. Everyone was travelling by the longer, inland route and the solitude increased Mileham's anxieties. He remembered Sir James Clyde's background; a mad father and a grandfather who had committed suicide. He remembered every word that Lawrence had told him, and everything he had discovered since their talk in the lounge. He suspected what the laird might be planning and the suspicion was unnerving.

Time to turn off now. The barrier Stuart and Richardson had encountered was less than a mile away and Mileham swung the

Land Rover on to a narrower and rougher road on his left. A track that zigzagged up the hillside, and now and then was as steep as the roof of a gable. Though he had put the transmission into four-wheel drive, Mileham was not young and he had to struggle to keep control of the van. The tyres lurched over loose stones and gravel and more than once he almost skidded over the precipices that plunged to the sea. He was so intent on driving that he never saw the three men flagging him down, and the roar of the engine drowned their hails.

A long, hard slog under the hot afternoon sun. He was dripping with sweat before he reached the head of the pass, but the journey had been worthwhile, and when he finally stopped and switched off the ignition the view was spectacular. To the west the crater of Ben Sagur soared blue and amber in the shimmering light. On his right he could just see the Glen of Tarbert and Liskerg village crouched in the shadow on a smaller mountain. In clear view lay the main road and the barrier that had been described to him. Barbed wire was stretched between two trees and men were stationed before it, while other men patrolled the adjacent fields.

Mileham had brought a twelve-bore shotgun and a pair of bin-oculars with him and he slung them both over his shoulder after he climbed out from the driving seat. The gun was not intended for use as a weapon, but as a camouflage, and if he was spotted he'd have a plausible excuse for his presence on the hills. They swarmed with grouse and blackcock, and the Red Deer was noted for its game-pies. 'Nothing to worry about, Sir James,' would be the report to the laird. 'Only old Mickey Mileham after a few brace, and you gave him shooting permission.'

A fair excuse – almost as fair as the foreman's, but when he raised the binoculars to his eyes and the distant scene came into focus, he knew that it wouldn't work. What he saw suggested that Lawrence's worst fears were justified and he lowered the glasses and hurried back to the van.

There was a button concealed under the dashboard; when Mileham pressed it a panel slid back to reveal a radio transmitter, and a tall aerial snaked up into the almost windless sky. He took a notebook from his pocket, prepared to jot down a coded Morse

transcript, and then changed his mind. Time was vital and the
message for Lawrence must be sent in plain language. He plugged
in a microphone lead and switched on the set.

Michael Mileham; hotelier, spy, informer and patriot spoke into
the microphone for exactly one minute and thirty-eight seconds
before the men he had failed to notice came running towards him
and opened fire.

Like little Mary Alison he had finished his journey, delivered the
goods and kept a date with death, the Last Enemy.

# Three

'Strange how long-lived this stuff is, Bill.' Sir Marcus Levin, K.C.B.,
F.R.S. and winner of a Nobel prize for services to medicine,
frowned at Colonel William Lawrence who lay stretched out on
the consulting-room couch. 'Only heat and acid can destroy it.'
Mark picked up a pair of scissors and started to snip at Lawrence's
thick mat of chest hair, which was hindering his examination.

'Tom Cuthbert, the civil engineer, showed me a rather
gruesome spectacle the other day. His firm are preparing the foundations for a tower block in north London and the men broke into
a seventeenth-century plague pit. As might be expected, most of
the bodies were only skeletons and their clothes had rotted away.
But the hair had survived. After more than three hundred years it
had not even faded and I saw every possible shade of colour from
black to white.' Mark worked away to remove the tenacious fibres.
'One chap was gingery-grey like yourself.'

'Very interesting, Mark, but I didn't come to the hospital to hear
reminiscences.' Lawrence was full of anxiety, impatience and self-
pity. 'Just what is wrong with me?'

'We'll know when they've checked your blood sample and the
other specimens.' Mark's barbering was completed and he held his
lens over a mottled expanse of flesh. 'But let me finish the story,
because it could concern you personally.

'Four of the corpses in that pit were not skeletons. They had
been buried at the edge of a peat belt and were almost perfectly

preserved. I could even recognize the symptoms of their illness. The buboes and the plague spots; a rash rather similar to your own in its early stages.'

'Good God, Mark! You don't . . . You can't imagine . . .' Though Lawrence had once stormed a Japanese machine-gun post single-handed, he stared at his medical adviser in abject terror. 'The rash is irritating, I am feeling under the weather; but plague! Hell's bells, I haven't been out of the British Isles for years.'

'That's no guarantee of safety, Bill. This country has experienced two of the worst plague epidemics in history.' Mark had seen enough and he grinned and walked over to a wash-basin. 'No, of course you're not suffering from *bacillus pestis*. If there was a chance of that you'd be on your way to an isolation ward already.' He soaped his hands while he spoke. 'In my view, the rash is not even an infection and I'm confident the lab will confirm that diagnosis.' Mark had finished washing and he looked at his watch. 'We should have the report at any moment, so get dressed and relax.'

'Not an infection, you say.' Lawrence pulled on his shirt, but he was far from relaxed and his fingers fumbled clumsily with the buttons. 'Then why am I off-colour and what's causing those damn spots?'

'I think that should tell us.' An intercom on Mark's desk was buzzing and he pressed a switch. 'Levin here.'

'Ah, good afternoon, Sir Marcus, and it really is a good one for late September.' The speaker's voice was full of jovial benevolence and one could almost imagine that Mr Pickwick was on the line. 'Makes me feel as cheerful as a cricket.'

'I'm delighted to hear it, Dr Godspel.' Mark glanced through the window. The weather was heavy and oppressive and he couldn't see anything to cheer about. 'Have you tested those specimens I sent over, Doctor? The patient is with me now and he's rather worried about his condition.'

'Then you can tell the poor, dear man to stop worrying, Sir Marcus.' Godspel obviously enjoyed delivering good news. 'In fact, worry is probably the cause of his trouble, because all my findings are reassuring. Sugar and albumen content fairly normal, no cholesterol buildup to speak of, no evidence of attack by micro-organisms. That should relieve his mind, eh.'

'I'm sure it will and many thanks, Dr Godspel.'

'Not at all, Sir Marcus. Always a pleasure to work with you; also to meet you socially. Kate and I are very much looking forward to our date tomorrow evening.'

'As we are, Doctor.' Mark lied because he had forgotten the unwelcome dinner invitation. 'Seven-thirty for eight, I think you said, so goodbye till then.

'My diagnosis appears to be confirmed, Bill.' He had switched off the set and turned to Lawrence. 'Your rash is not an infection; it's psychosomatic. A nervous condition due to anxiety, overwork and over-indulgence and I intended to frighten you.' He eyed his patient sternly. The colonel was a stout, bag-eyed man with a tanned complexion that had been produced more by alcohol than by sun and wind.

'You work too hard and you worry too much. You also eat, drink and smoke far too much and, if you hadn't got the consti-tution of an ox, you'd be dead.' Mark pulled his prescription-pad from a drawer. 'These tranquillizers should calm you down and I'll give you an ointment for the rash. You'll be all right in a day or two, but the condition will return unless you look after yourself, Bill. You must go easy on every count I mentioned.'

'Which will be damned difficult, old boy.' Now that he knew he wasn't suffering from plague, Lawrence felt slightly more cheerful, though only slightly. 'I suppose I can cut down on the grub and the booze, but I'm a compulsive smoker, and if you knew how worry-ing my job was . . .'

'I do know. You're in the Internal Security Service, so naturally your work is exacting.' Mark wrote out the prescriptions. 'But we all have professional worries and the trick is to confine them to office hours.' If Mark Levin had such worries, he did not show them. He looked supremely assured and self-confident and much younger than his forty-odd years. 'Pick these up at a chemist and take one of the tablets before lunch. A frugal lunch, Bill; boiled fish or salad. No aperitifs – no wine – no liqueurs.'

'Thanks, Mark.' Lawrence was fully dressed and he slipped the prescription into his wallet. 'That fellow who did the tests – what's he like?'

'Edgar Godspel?' The question surprised Mark and he hesitated before replying. 'A rum bird. I suppose Hail-Fellow-Well-Met might be an apt description. Over-benevolent, over-jovial, with a hulking battleship of a wife who bullies him, and an irritating sense of humour. Godspel would spend his last penny to buy a hungry man a meal and then spoil the gesture by popping a rubber frog into his soup. As you heard, Tania and I are dining with the Godspels tomorrow and I'm not looking forward to it one little bit.' Mark grimaced at the prospect.

'They'll probably offer us seats that blow raspberries when we sit on them. Edgar Godspel is a boring, good-humoured practical joker and also bone idle. With his brains and qualifications he could hold down an important research post, but he's buried himself here at St Bede's. An analyst in a general hospital.

'But I can assure you that Godspel doesn't joke about our patients and that report will be a hundred per cent accurate. Why did you ask about him, Bill?'

'Because the name's uncommon and I came across a Godspel once. Had to interview him in the course of business.' Though Lawrence was craving for a cigarette, he heeded Mark's warning. 'A rather sinister incident and I suppose it can't be the same chap.'

'Unlikely. I can't imagine our Godspel getting up to anything sinister. But what is the matter?' Lawrence had joined him at the desk and Mark saw that he was scowling at a copy of *Life and History Magazine*. A photograph of a man in highland dress was displayed on the cover and there was a quoted statement below it. 'I am the arch-enemy of central governments – I am proud to be their enemy.'

'He's the matter, Mark, and you tell me to relax.' Discretion vanished and the colonel opened his cigarette case. 'That bastard happens to be one of my major headaches at the moment.'

'Why on earth should he be?' Mark had only skimmed through the first part of the article. 'I thought James Clyde was a public benefactor. A brilliant businessman who had trebled his inherited fortune and was spending the money developing a backward area.

'I'm also rather sympathetic towards his political views. Centralized government does cramp local initiative, and by all accounts he's done a lot for his people. Full employment, new schools and . . .'

'And pictures of himself in every public building and place of entertainment.' Lawrence's voice was tired and irritable. 'Sir James Fraser Clyde has made himself the virtual dictator of a Scottish county, and he creates work to gain popularity and allegiance. Crackpot schemes to raise a treasure ship and to find gold in an extinct volcano.' The colonel lit a cigarette and inhaled deeply. 'Projects that are smoke-screens with a pretty odd lot of technicians engaged on them. Mainly foreigners, and I'd wager a year's salary that half of them are ex-Nazis, I.R.A. men and fugitives from the O.A.S. Clyde also has a private army, and the schools you mentioned are staffed by teachers who preach his gospel. "Scotland's future – Scottish independence – the need for Scotland to have a strong leader."'

'A private army and ex-Nazis?' Mark was beginning to appreciate his friend's concern. 'If you're sure about this, why can't something be done, Bill? There must be police in the area.'

'Most of the local police are in Clyde's pocket, and I am not sure, I merely suspect. Without definite evidence what can be done? Sending troops into Northern Ireland was one of the worst blunders a British Government ever made, in my opinion, and there've been no complaints about Clyde. His people revere him, and unless we discover what he's really up to, he must be left alone.

'What do I think he's up to?' Lawrence took a second drag at the cigarette before answering Mark's question. 'Again, I only suspect, but judging from his parentage and present activities, it seems probable that Sir James is building something pretty nasty in his woodshed.'

'Parentage?' Mark raised his eyebrows. 'Yes, I remember hearing about that. The father died in a madhouse believing he was God.

'Excuse me though.' The telephone had rung and he picked it up. 'Extension 135.

'Yes, he's with me now.' He held the receiver out to Lawrence.

'Your secretary, Bill. More disturbing affairs of state I presume.'

'Could be. I gave her your number in case something urgent cropped up.' Lawrence shrugged as he lifted the instrument. 'Hullo, Marjorie.

'A message from Mickey Mileham, eh. Anything interesting?

'What – what's that?' The colonel's face had become dark-red as he listened. 'Just repeat exactly what he said before the transmission ended, Marjorie. I want to hear every single word . . .

'Then the sod may have finally gone and done it.' Though Lawrence's face was dark, his knuckles were white above the telephone. 'No, I don't know what action should be taken, but I bloody well know what I'd like to do. Send in every available bomber and blast that mountain to rubble.' He paused to consider the situation.

'An impossible solution unfortunately, so just inform the police and the Special Branch and Scottish Command that something is in the offing. Don't give them too many details though. Hotheads might panic and take the law into their own hands if you're too precise.

'We must be certain that Mileham's information is accurate, and though bombers are out, General Blackhurst had better lay on a helicopter reconnaissance immediately.

'Finally, I must see Lord Osenton as soon as possible. Call his office straight away and then get back to me at this number.' Lawrence slammed down the phone and leaned heavily against the desk.

'Talk of the devil as much as you like, Mark,' he said. 'Tell me that coincidences rarely happen, but don't – please don't order me to relax.

'Oh, very well.' He saw the eagerness in Mark's face and shrugged again. 'I'll put you in the picture, but keep it to yourself till the balloon goes up. An event which may soon be forthcoming.' He glowered at the cover photograph of Sir James Clyde, the Smilin' Boy, and sighed.

'It seems likely that this joker is about to test an atom bomb.'

'According to my calculations we must be well over the peninsula now, Skipper.' Flight-Sergeant Peter (Pussy) Palmer peered out of the throbbing helicopter, but the weather had changed for the worse and all he could see was a grey carpet of mist. 'I thought I caught a glimpse of Liskerg a while back, though the cloud's too thick to be sure.'

'Thank you, Sergeant, but I much prefer *sir* or my official title to *skipper*. We are not on board a herring trawler.' Normally a flying officer would have been at the helicopter's controls, but for this expedition, the exalted personage of Squadron-Leader the Honourable Gerald Chadwyck had assumed command, and he was a stickler for protocol. 'Keep your eyes skinned, because we'll be going down soon.'

'Will do, sir,' Palmer replied humbly through his helmet microphone. But, 'you toffee-nosed bastard,' he said to himself and considered their orders which had been delivered by a Group Captain and a visiting Major General.

'Apparently Clyde's set up some kind of cordon, so maintain a good ceiling till you're well over the area and then make a thorough inspection.' The Group Captain had tapped a map. 'Land if necessary, because we must know what's happening in those mountains.'

'Try not to be spotted, however. Colonel Lawrence's signal was pretty vague, but there may be some rough customers on the prowl, chaps. A force of nationalist irregulars run on the lines of the I.R.A.' Unlike Chadwyck, the General seemed to be a decent old buffer with a democratic approach. 'For that reason you will both be issued with small arms and you have my full authority to use them should the need arise.'

'Right, Sergeant.' Chadwyck's clipped voice rasped through the earphones. 'Keep a good lookout, because I am making the descent.'

'My eyes are as bare as peeled onions, Squadron-Leader.' The aircraft had dropped into the cloud and Palmer was blinded by the layers of moisture. 'But I still don't know what we're supposed to be looking for.'

'You were present at the briefing, man, and General Blackhurst made it quite clear that he wasn't sure himself.' Chadwyck didn't bother to conceal his impatience. 'We were told to inspect the Ben Sagur range and report anything out of the way. Any abnormal activity or lack of it. Anything strange or exceptional. Is that understood?'

'I suppose so, sir, but . . .' They were almost under the cloud belt and through its wisps Palmer could make out the terrain. A wild, inhospitable country of rocks and streams and heather.

'There's a village over to starboard, Squadron-Leader. About three miles away, so should we make a check?'

'I don't see why.' Chadwyck's impatience increased. 'Our orders were to reconnoitre the mountains. Villages are no concern of ours.'

'This one might be, sir.' Palmer was peering through a pair of binoculars. 'We're supposed to report anything unusual and I think there's something pretty queer about that dump.'

'Very well.' The sergeant had sounded excited, and against his personal wishes Chadwyck lowered the altitude and swung the helicopter to the right. They had been told to keep the reconnaissance as discreet as possible but once over the village their presence must be noted.

'Yes, I see what you mean, Palmer.' The aircraft was hovering above the buildings and he shared the sergeant's excitement; though 'village' was a grandiose description. A mere hamlet with a few dozen houses clustered around a small church. An unusual hamlet however, because there was no sign of activity. Nobody was visible in the streets, no children ran out of the doors to stare at them, no vehicles moved. The place seemed completely deserted and it made Chadwyck think of a disused film set.

'Signal to base and tell 'em that . . .' he consulted his map – 'that Glenreach village appears to have been evacuated.' Chadwyck watched Palmer switch on the transmitter and then headed towards Ben Sagur. Mist was drifting down from the mountain's summit, but the valley below was still clear and he saw two waterfalls pouring into a gorge to form a fair-sized river. A spectacular prospect for a landscape artist; though a sterile one.

'Not even a sheep in sight.' The loneliness was affecting Chadwyck and his lordly manner vanished. 'Like a close-up of the moon. It gives me the creeps.'

'Me too, sir.' Palmer had completed his message and was craning out of the cockpit. 'But could you go a bit lower? My sight may be packing up, but I don't believe those things by the stream are boulders.'

'There's nothing wrong with your eyesight.' Chadwyck had seen what Palmer was looking at and at first he'd tried to pretend that his own eyes were deceiving him. But only for a moment, and he remembered the Group Captain's orders. 'I'm going to land Sergeant, so cross your fingers.' Very reluctantly he slowed the engine revs and brought the helicopter down on a marshy strip at the head of the valley.

'A massacre, sir . . . a bloody massacre.' The two men had removed their helmets and climbed out. Palmer spoke in whispers. Viewed from the air it had seemed possible that the objects might have been grotesquely shaped rocks, but at close quarters there was no doubt. They were real enough – real and horrible, and they lay stretched out in attitudes of agony.

'Why, sir?' Palmer had served in Cyprus and Northern Ireland and believed that no display of brutality could surprise him. But he had never imagined witnessing such a scene on a peaceful Scottish hillside. 'Who could have done it?'

'God knows, though they must have used flamethrowers.' The fog was getting thicker, spiralling from the crags above, and Chadwyck opened his camera-case to photograph the remains displayed before them. Partially burned human corpses; the charred bodies of men and women and children left to rot on the sodden turf. As Palmer had said, the victims of a massacre.

'Look at her, Pussy.' Protocol had gone to the winds and Chadwyck was staring at the face of a dead girl. 'Look at her features.' He lowered the camera and fought back the urge to vomit.

'Christ – Jesus Christ.' Palmer also felt sick, but nausea was replaced by panic and he swung round. 'What's that, sir? That noise?' The helicopter was ticking over and a third sound had joined the throb of its engine and the roar of the waterfalls. A faint, distant sound at first, but growing louder second by second. An obscene sound full of threat and menace. A sound which terrified him. 'Can't you hear it, Skipper?'

'Of course I can.' Chadwyck reached for the automatic pistol in the pocket of his flying-jacket. 'And just for a moment I thought I saw something. Something coming towards us.

'Yes, there – there – there. There it is, and we're cut off from the chopper.' He raised the pistol and fired wildly into the swirling mist.

From in front of them and from behind them, to the right and the left of them the sound increased. The same sound Mary Alison had heard in her grandmother's cottage. A sound which might have been made by pigs guzzling swill.

## Four

'One man – one power-drunk, egocentric man – with unlimited force at his disposal; an unnerving prospect, old boy.' Three hours had gone by; Mark Levin was at home pacing the floor of his library and considering what Lawrence had told him.

'James Clyde is unbalanced and the condition is probably hereditary,' Lawrence had said. 'Both his father and grandfather showed early traces of genius and then went potty. But Clyde is not insane enough to imagine gold-prospecting on Ben Sagur could be profitable, and for some time I've suspected his reason for starting those mining operations. That message from our chap in Scotland appears to confirm my fears.' Lawrence had stubbed out a cigarette and immediately lighted another before stating what he had learned.

And Bill Lawrence's fears were probably justified, Mark thought. With scientific knowledge and financial resources it was not difficult to construct an atomic device and Clyde had both. He was a multi-millionaire and it seemed that many of his technicians were physicists. The difficulty was not the production of a prototype bomb, but the testing of it, and that explained the excavations.

If the crater of an extinct volcano was deepened, the shaft could contain the explosion, but the shock waves would be recorded for hundreds of miles and the world informed that there was another major power to reckon with. Not a nation or a government to be deterred by fear of reprisal, but a single individual with terms to dictate – his own terms. 'Do what I say, or I'll blow your house down.'

'I haven't a clue what those terms will be, Mark.' Lawrence had produced a flask from his pocket and knocked back a mouthful of neat brandy. 'But if the test is successful, we'll know soon enough, and this is what our man reported before they killed or wounded him.'

Soon enough! Mark lifted an atlas from a bookshelf and opened it at a map of western Scotland. The Ben Sagur peninsula jutted some twenty miles out into the Atlantic and was less than six miles wide where it joined the mainland. Not a difficult area to screen off, and Mark tried to picture what Lawrence's agent had seen before the rattle of gunfire interrupted his message. A miniature Iron Curtain of stakes and barbed wire and armed men on patrol.

And behind the barrier, a village which appeared to be completely deserted. Sir James Clyde had not only sealed the peninsula. He had evacuated the inhabitants, and everything added up.

'Damn you, Clyde,' Mark muttered aloud, closing the atlas and looking at the magazine he'd brought home from the hospital. The man on its cover was handsome at first glance and the twinkling eyes and curved mouth accounted for his nickname. But, like Michael Mileham, Mark saw that the eyes were wrong; and not only the eyes. The lips were narrow and cruel and there was no charity in the laird's expression. The Smilin' Boy had a sense of humour . . . one couldn't deny him that. He would smile at a crucifixion.

'Damn you, Sir James Fraser Clyde,' Mark repeated, quite oblivious of his wife who was bent over a newspaper. 'May you and all your fellow megalomaniacs rot in hell.'

'What is the matter, darling?' Tania Levin looked up and frowned. She was a tall, fair girl with a thin, soulful face and a sensuous figure. A contrast which sometimes made Mark think that two women were sharing the same house. A pious madonna upstairs and a plump earth-mother bulging out of the ground floor and basement. 'I don't mind you stalking around like a caged tiger, but talking to yourself is a bit much.

'And who are you condemning to eternal torment?' She nodded

at the paper which stated that Palestinian terrorists had sabotaged an Israeli airliner causing heavy loss of life. 'These fanatics?'

'No, not them.' Mark shook his head. 'They're murderous thugs, but they won't break my people, because we're the world's champion survivors. We survived Pharaoh and the Romans, Torquemada and the Tsars and the Nazis, and we'll survive the Arabs.

'Sorry if I'm on edge, Tania, but I've had a hard day.' Though Mark longed to tell her the truth he'd promised to respect Lawrence's confidence. 'I've also been reminded about our date tomorrow and I'm not looking forward to it. Edgar Godspel's *bonhommeries* at the hospital are bad enough, but a whole evening of them may be pretty trying.'

'Poor Mark.' Tania reached out and fondled his hand. 'Personally, I rather like the Godspels. He can be quite amusing when he hasn't had too much to drink, and she's not a bad old stick; though stick's no way to describe a woman who must top the scales at sixteen stone.

'I've often wondered about Edgar Godspel's drinking. Usually he's as sober as judges are supposed to be, but every so often he hits the bottle and makes a fool of himself. Have you any idea why?'

'God knows, though for some reason it always seems to be around this time of year, so let's hope that he's sober tomorrow.' Mark had more to worry about than his colleague's alcohol problem and he moved away from Tania and looked at the magazine photograph again.

Yes, a handsome face on the surface, he thought. The face of a brave and brilliant man. James Clyde had not only trebled his family fortune and won his tenants' loyalty. He held honours degrees in history and physics and earned a D.S.O. and a Military Cross when he was in Korea. But also the face of a megalomaniac, whose father had died raving. Possibly the face of a psychopath incapable of fear, pity, or remorse.

'God does know.' Mark repeated the phrase silently. 'God knows everything, so damn him, God. If Bill Lawrence is right, damn Clyde and all his crazy kind to hell.'

'Damn them – damn the weak, incompetent fools.' Sir James Alistair Fraser Clyde also had reason to curse. He stood on the ridge where Michael Mileham had died, and like Mileham he was scanning the landscape through a pair of binoculars. He wore a British military greatcoat over his kilt. A revolver of British manufacture hung from a belt at his side, and he spoke English with only the slightest trace of a Scottish accent.

'Is the barrier secure, Hans?' His glasses swept over the line of barbed-wire entanglements below the hillside and then he raised them to the west. The sun was going down, Ben Sagur was obscured by thick, black cloud and rain was on the way. 'Really secure?'

'As secure as possible, but we have too few men available.' Hans Weber's own guttural accent betrayed his country of origin. 'So when, Jaimie? When will you come to a decision and make an announcement? In my opinion it must be soon.'

'Your opinion is unimportant, Hans, and the decision is mine – mine alone.' Now that the sun was setting it was bitterly cold on the hill, but the temperature didn't make Clyde shiver inside his plaid and his heavy coat. 'I started this business and I shall finish it, whatever the cost.'

'As you say, but . . .' Weber's second question was not completed because Clyde had lowered the binoculars and the German stifled a gasp as he saw his chief's eyes. They were as arrogant as ever, but a little nervous tic trembled beneath each of them. Hans Weber had served the laird for a long time, and worshipped him as he had once worshipped a more famous fanatic. But he knew that the Smilin' Boy was approaching breaking point.

'We shall wait till morning in any case, Hans, and let's hope that Andy Martin has encouraging news.' Clyde watched a motorcycle climbing up from the plain. 'If not, I shall do what must be done. The responsibility belongs to me – just as the people and the land and the dream belong to me.' He closed his eyes for a moment and then opened them wide when the bicycle topped the crest and chugged to a halt.

'Well, Andy?' Clyde stepped forward as the rider dismounted and gave a weary salute. 'You have been gone for two hours. You must have covered the entire perimeter, so what can you tell us?'

'Nothing, sir; nothing at all.' The man's helmet and face-shield were in position and he spoke in gasps. 'The area is dead; as empty as a desert and you can relax.'

'Thank you.' Though Clyde smiled automatically, his muscles tensed. Over the years he had developed an almost telepathic warning device and its signal rang out like an alarm bell. 'Good news, but I want a detailed report from you, Andy, so take off your helmet and show me the exact route you took.' There was a map-case in Clyde's pocket, but he did not reach for it. His hand moved towards the gun hanging from his belt, and he repeated himself sharply.

'I told you to remove your helmet.' The order was obeyed, the tell-tale signs were revealed and Sir James Clyde grabbed the pistol and pressed the trigger.

'Sorry about that, Andy,' he said after the six chambers were empty and the man lay dead on the ground. 'My fault – all mine.'

'Yes, all mine.' He smiled at his victim, but it was another automatic smile. The Smilin' Boy had nothing to smile about.

## Five

Edgar Godspel lived in a pleasant, modern bungalow beside the Thames with a lawn running down to the water's edge. A trim, well-kept lawn, apart from one blemish. The light shining from the sitting-room window revealed a circle of blackened turf.

'What caused that, Mrs Godspel?' Though the Levins had known the Godspels for some time, their relationship remained formal and neither couple had chosen to adopt first names.

'Children, Sir Marcus.' She pointed at a block of slum-clearance flats. 'Since the council built that monstrosity, the district has been plagued by teenage vandals. When we were out one evening last month, a gang of them came across the river in a boat and lit a bonfire. Infuriating, though I suppose we were lucky that they didn't break into the premises. Three of our neighbours have been burgled recently and there've been countless other acts of hooliganism. How I'd love to get my hands on the little beasts.'

'I don't blame you.' Mark sympathized with his hostess, but also felt concern for her potential victims. Kathleen Godspel was a powerful, heavily-built woman with long, jet-black hair and a craggy face made slightly sinister by a pair of thick-rimmed pebble glasses.

'Why don't you buy a dog? I've always heard that they're the best deterrent.' While he spoke, Mark was considering another deterrent. The fear of reprisal for atomic attack. A deterrent which would be meaningless if the power to attack belonged to a single maniac.

'Because I detest dogs almost as much as children, Sir Marcus. Noisy, insanitary brutes and I wouldn't have one in the house.'

'Then what's the matter with a kennel, my dear?' Edgar Godspel was the physical opposite of his wife. A bald, gnome-like man who collected antique fire-arms and jokes. The walls of the room were hung with flintlock muskets and pistols, and a joke was clearly in the offing. 'But not to worry about your dislike of the canine species, Kate. As W. C. Fields said, "There can't be much wrong with anybody who hates children and dawgs."' The impersonation was a flop, but it showed that the doctor was getting into his stride. No raspberry-blowing cushions had been provided to regale Mark and Tania and he'd drunk sparingly before and during the meal. But after leaving the table, he'd downed several glasses of port and his eyes had the gleam of the habitual storyteller. 'And talking of kennels, do you know the one about the bishop who had a crush on a Great Dane?'

'I'm sure they do, Edgar,' Kathleen Godspel interposed firmly. 'I certainly do and found it quite funny on the first dozen tellings.'

'Then I won't tell it again.' Though the little man smiled, the sneer had obviously embarrassed him and he crossed over to Tania, who was looking at a photograph on the mantelpiece. 'Isn't she pretty, Lady Levin?'

'Extremely pretty.' Tania nodded, but her reply was a half-truth. The picture showed the head and shoulders of a girl in her twenties, and though the sitter was certainly beautiful, she couldn't really be called pretty. The face was too intelligent, the expression too hard; handsome was an apter description. 'Your daughter, Dr Godspel?'

'Oh no, Kathleen and I have only been married for a few years and she would be almost thirty now.' His voice was slightly wistful. 'Just a friend we lost contact with.'

'I see.' There was something familiar about the face and Tania searched her memory. 'But I've got a feeling that I know her. At least that I've met her at some time.'

'You probably saw her picture in the newspapers, Lady Levin.' Kathleen Godspel was pouring Mark another cup of coffee. 'The case became quite a *cause célèbre* for a while.

'Who on earth can that be?' The telephone was ringing and she lowered the coffee-pot and glanced at her watch. 'Twenty to eleven! What an ungodly hour to phone.'

'8925 . . . 7835.' She announced the number irritably and then frowned. 'Yes – yes, he is here. Hang on please.' She held the receiver out to Mark. 'A Colonel Lawrence for you, Sir Marcus, and he says it's urgent.'

'Thank you.' Mark recalled telling Lawrence he would be dining with the Godspels, but he couldn't imagine a reason for the call. 'Good evening Bill.'

'It's not a good evening, old boy.' The Colonel's voice was brusque and impatient. 'It's a bloody bad one, and I'm afraid you'll have to cut short your dinner-party. There'll be a car round to pick you up in a few moments, because an invitation . . . a royal command has been issued and you're included in the list of guests.

'No, I can't go into details. I don't really know any, though I will say this.' Mark had questioned him and Lawrence's tone became even brusquer. 'At our last meeting I told you that the balloon could be going up, and it appears I was right.' Lawrence might have been speaking from a station call-box with his eye on the clock and a train to catch. 'The balloon is going up and we need you. It may just be one of your own balloons.'

*　★　*

One of your own balloons! What could the statement mean, Mark wondered as the car rushed him out through the London suburbs – a police car, which had arrived almost as soon as Lawrence

had rung off and he'd told Tania and the Godspels that he had to
leave.

'I'm sorry, sir, but I'm quite in the dark myself.' The driver was
a young constable who spoke slowly and sparingly, but drove as
though he was on a race-track. 'I was instructed to deliver you
to an address beyond Strenton and to get there as soon as possible. Clanross Grange the place is called, and that's all I know.' He
had fallen silent and concentrated on obeying his orders; weaving
skilfully through the thin, late-night traffic and sounding the siren
whenever a roundabout or a road junction came into sight.

One of your own balloons? Again and again Mark considered
the statement. Bill Lawrence was worried by the possibility that
an unbalanced Scottish landowner had managed to produce an
atomic weapon. How could that concern him; except as a potential victim? He was a hunter of germs; one of the world's foremost
experts in bacteriology, but any first-year physics student could
match his knowledge of nuclear fission. Mark Levin did not suffer
from false modesty or conceit. He knew his value; he knew his
limitations; so why did Lawrence need him? What use could he be?

It wouldn't be long before he found out. They had roared
through Strenton village, and for the first time since leaving Godspel's bungalow, the driver hesitated.

'Should be somewhere on the left, I think, sir.' He had switched
on the headlamps and was peering through their beam. 'Yes, this
must be it.' He stamped on the brake pedal, but the car was still
travelling too fast for comfort and Mark was jerked against his
seat-belt as they swung through a pair of wrought-iron gates. 'A
bit creepy, eh?'

'It certainly is, officer.' The drive was long and narrow and pit-
ted with ruts. Dying elm trees flanked it on one side; on the other,
a graveyard. The private cemetery of a proud, wealthy family,
which must have been imposing before neglect allowed nature to
take over. The lights showed that the granite obelisks were covered
with grime and lichen. Brambles sprouted around the rusty rail-
ings of the tombs, and other vegetation partially obscured marble
urns and crosses and angels. Even under a bright sun the scene
would have been gloomy. At night it was the epitome of depres-

sion and Mark tried to visualize the kind of people who had buried their dead in a front garden.

'I'll be handing you over to Dracula in a moment, sir.' The constable chuckled, because the house looming before them was grimmer than its grounds. A crumbling, Jacobean mansion long overdue for demolition. Though one or two of the windows glowed with light, some of them lacked glass, part of the roof had caved in and a length of loose guttering sagged over the pretentious porch. The driver could be right about Count Dracula, Mark thought jokingly as the car drew up beside a group of parked vehicles – and then his body went rigid. Bill Lawrence was also right. Coincidences did happen.

'There you are, Sir Marcus.' A man in a neat black suit had strutted from the porch and opened Mark's door. 'This is a pleasure, sir; an honour. My name is Hans Weber and, though we have never met, I naturally know of you by reputation.'

'No, we have never met, Mr Weber – not socially.' The strutting walk had aroused Mark's suspicions and he climbed from the car, ignoring the outstretched hand and studying the man's face. An old face now. The hair was white, but the features had not altered significantly and there was still the familiar 'V' shaped scar on the chin. While he looked at that scar, the years seemed to roll back and Mark became a boy again. A small, frightened boy, cowering in a barbed-wire compound. He remembered the day his parents had been arrested. He remembered the Battle of the Warsaw Ghetto and the Ruhr labour camps. He remembered Belsen and a place called Ruhleben.

He also remembered the neatly dressed figure leading the way towards the ruined house, though he'd never known his real name and never seen him in civilian clothes.

Why should he have done? The man who'd introduced himself as Hans Weber had always worn uniform on duty and had always been addressed by his official title. As was right and proper, because he was an important person with an important job.

An S. S. Sturmführer and the commandant of a concentration camp.

# Six

Hans Weber was a bad man and the house was a bad house. Mark sensed that as soon as he stepped into the entrance hall and his feelings were not caused by the building's dilapidated condition. The smell of damp and wood rot . . . the floor soft and spongy under his feet . . . the rat holes in the skirting boards . . . the cobwebs festooning the peeling wallpaper . . . the grey dust-sheets draped like shrouds over the furniture.

The house was old and neglected and mouldering, but decay didn't account for its atmosphere. If Clanross Grange had been redecorated and refurnished, if sunlight had been streaming through crystal-clear windows, the aura of evil would remain . . . the aura of its owners; the dead and the living.

'Please hurry, sir.' Mark had paused to glance around the hall and Weber beckoned him towards an open doorway. 'You are the last arrival and the others are waiting for you.'

'I'm coming . . . Mr Weber.' Mark was about to say, *Herr Sturmführer*, but he checked himself. The German had probably paid for his war crimes and Hitler was best forgotten. Recrimination was pointless and only the future mattered. A future which might be very grim indeed. He walked through the doorway and looked at his fellow guests.

The room had once been used as a chapel. It was as dilapidated as the hall, but the pews were still intact and a number of distinguished people occupied them. Mark recognized two Cabinet Ministers and Lord Osenton, the Premier's personal adviser. Professor Emily Repton from the government research station at Rushton Park, and Samuel Kahn, the Chairman of Global Newspapers. At the end of the first row was William Lawrence and a girl with a shorthand pad; presumably Lawrence's secretary.

'Will you take a seat, Sir Marcus?' Though the assembly was impressive, each individual looked anxious and cowed, and it was the man standing on the altar steps who dominated the scene.

Sir James Clyde's face was drawn with tiredness, and his kilt was rumpled as though he had been sleeping in it. But there was a mesmeric quality in his eyes which told Mark why his tenants worshipped him. How he had gained the loyalty of men like Hans Weber.

'First, let me apologize for your surroundings, ladies and gentlemen.' The hypnotic and not quite sane eyes swept over the benches. 'Clanross Grange has been unoccupied for a long time, but the house was once our English family home and it seemed appropriate that I make my announcement here.'

*My announcement*, Mark thought. Bill Lawrence is right. Clyde has produced an atom bomb and he's going to brag about it – to tell us exactly what his terms are. The presence of the Ministers and Osenton and Emily Repton and Kahn was explained. It was also clear why Lawrence was present. Those people were the Establishment; the rulers of the country. But Mark had one question he couldn't answer. Why had he been included?

'Next, let me admit to something Colonel Lawrence has suspected.' Clyde stepped up to a film screen positioned on the altar top. 'Rightly suspected, Colonel, and the messages we picked up from your agent, Michael Mileham, and an R.A.F. helicopter were quite accurate.' Clyde's voice was almost as magnetic as his eyes, but there was no threat in it. He didn't sound like a dictator delivering terms. He sounded like a confidence-trickster wheedling for a loan.

'Everything you suspected about me is correct, Colonel Lawrence. I do have a craving for power – a dream of my family's past greatness and Scotland's future greatness. I did try to turn that vision into reality and I nearly succeeded.' He nodded to Weber who was stationed beside a projector at the back of the room. The ceiling lights went out and a picture glowed on the screen. A technical diagram which meant nothing to Mark.

'I did employ scientists to produce an atomic device, Colonel. A weapon which would have made you and your masters cringe before me. "A fulcrum to move the world," and this was to be its birthplace.' He clicked his fingers and the diagram was replaced by a view of Ben Sagur.

'As your reports stated, this area has been cut off from the mainland, Colonel Lawrence, but not to explode our bombs. The tests were scheduled to take place later.' Though Clyde was invisible, there was personal spite towards Lawrence in his tone and Mark felt sure he was scowling.

'Yes, much later, but I'm talking too much.' He paused for a moment and, when he resumed, his voice was quite different. Warm and appealing and full of a rich, northern brogue.

'I've always been cursed over much with the gift of the gab and there's not time for chatter. We've got to face the facts and I hope yer'll no find them too disturbin'.

'As Rabbie Burns wrote, the best laid schemes o' mice an' men gang *aft a-gley*.' He chuckled, but the jocularity was false. Sir James Fraser Clyde was about to break, and if the room had not been in darkness his audience would have seen the agony in his twitching eyes as he bent to pull the dirk from his stocking. 'The ball's in your court, my friends. You're the official receivers . . . the lads and lassies who must pick up the pieces, and I . . . I'm a bankrupt.

'Sorry about the clichés – sorry about everything, but I can't go on any longer. You – you have to fight now. Fight the demons my folly created.' The words ended in a sound that might have been a curse or a cackle of laughter. The knife swung to its target but nobody noticed the Smilin' Boy's death. Before cutting his throat, Jaimie Clyde had clicked his fingers a second time and every eye was riveted on the final picture Hans Weber projected.

A distressing picture which produced several reactions and one verbal comment. Emily Repton and the Cabinet Ministers gasped. Lord Osenton grunted as though he had been punched in the stomach. William Lawrence stifled a curse. His secretary sighed.

But only Mark Levin knew what they were really looking at and he delivered his verdict in a single, hyphenated term.

'Lion-faced,' he said.

# Seven

'Lion-faced is a thickening of the features caused by certain dis-

THE FACE OF THE LION

eases, such as leprosy, but I never believed radiation could have the same effects. Apparently I was wrong.'

Twelve hours had passed since Sir James Clyde died. Ten since Hans Weber finished his personal testimony, and Mark was explaining the situation to Tania.

A disturbing situation, because Clyde and his associates really had released demons; legions of them. They had built a laboratory on the seaward side of Ben Sagur; they had tried to produce atomic devices and they had almost succeeded. One small bomb was to be exploded harmlessly in the mountain's artificially deepened crater to prove that the force was available. A second and much more powerful one planted in Clanross Grange – a threat to enforce Clyde's demands.

But before the work was completed, something went wrong. A technician with the commonplace name of Fred Brown became ill.

'Brown's symptoms resembled those of influenza,' Weber had said, standing beside his dead master who lay slumped below the altar. The news was too grim for anyone to bother about the Smilin' Boy, though a dust sheet had been draped over his body.

'Brown complained of headaches and a sore throat, and he was running a temperature. It seemed clear that flu was his trouble and there was no suspicion of radiation. He was ordered to bed, but he didn't stay there long. Fred Brown vanished. He wandered off into the country and within a short time other people became contaminated.

'They looked like this.' Weber had moved back to the projector and Mark winced at the memory of the things projected on the screen. Though dead and charred, their lifetime deformities were still horribly visible.

'Radiation didn't kill them, Tania. They killed each other and Clyde decided not to inform the authorities. He cordoned off the area and ordered his thugs – his private army – to shoot the survivors and burn their corpses with flame-throwers. Poor, mad, irresponsible fool.'

Though Mark spoke savagely, he wasn't sure that his anger was justified. The outbreak was unlike anything he had experienced or heard about, and more than physical changes were involved. Mental aberrations took place, and *demons* was not an exaggerated description of creatures whose aims were destruction and the spread of their complaint. An old woman had strangled her granddaughter. Men and women and children had hurled themselves against the barbed-wire barriers in efforts to attack Clyde's guards. The crew of a helicopter had been murdered – torn apart by deformed, half-human hands.

A complaint which spread quickly. In the hope that the epidemic was over, Clyde had sent a dispatch rider to inspect the area and in just two hours the man had returned with the symptoms clear on his face. That was what had made Clyde finally accept defeat. Why he had finally appealed for help. Why he had cut his throat in shame and remorse, believing that his experiments were entirely responsible.

'The urge to transmit your illness to another person is a common enough phenomenon, Tania. Intercourse with a virgin was once regarded as a cure for syphilis.' Mark recalled another instance of the belief; a passage from Pepys' account of the London plague, telling how *sick people would breathe in the faces of well people passing by.*

But syphilis and plague had no bearing on the subject. Disease was caused by parasites – viruses and bacteria and other microorganisms. Could radiation produce the same effects; mental and physical? Could it be infectious?

In any case, time would tell. The army and its medical corps were replacing Clyde's irregulars, and a team of experts from Rushton Park research establishment had been sent to examine the prototype bomb. That was logical, but why – just why – had Clyde wanted him to be present at the meeting?

Why – why – why? Again and again Mark asked himself the question. Sir James Fraser Clyde was dead. He couldn't provide an answer and neither could Hans Weber. All Weber knew was that Clyde had telephoned Lawrence and named the people he wanted to talk to.

Emily Repton was a physicist. Her knowledge was invaluable, and it was also obvious why the ministers and Lord Osenton and

Samuel Kahn had been present. Clyde had needed scientific help and public support to fight an outbreak of nuclear radiation, but how could a bacteriologist help him? What advice could he, Mark Levin, offer?

'Perhaps Clyde suspected that it wasn't radiation, darling.' Tania had read his thoughts. She had also read the article in *Life and History* and opened the magazine at a subheading, SEARCH FOR THE DOOMED GALLEON. 'They never found the ship,' she said, pointing at a photograph. 'They found this.'

'The *Santa Veronica* galleon, Sir Marcus?' Admiral Archibald Fetherstone, curator of the London Maritime Museum, liked the sound of his own voice and it boomed from the telephone as though issuing orders in the teeth of a gale. 'Naturally I know all about her. I produced a television programme on the subject not so long ago. My knowledge is exhaustive on all matters pertaining to ships and the sea.

'A rum yarn, though if you're considering investing in James Clyde's salvage venture, I'd advise you to hang on to your money and put it into a building society. Although there are a number of ignorant and ill-informed opinions, the *Veronica* may have been carrying treasure, but I'll bet my bottom dollar that the crafty Scots got their hands on it before scuttling her.

'Oh yes, she was scuttled all right. Whatever journalists, hack writers and jumped-up dons claiming to be historians, may say, there's no doubt about that in my view.' The admiral made it clear that his view was the only one which mattered.

'The *Santa Veronica* was a large, four-decked vessel, commanded by a certain Don Francesco Valdes and she fled from Calais with the rest of the Armada fleet and beat her way round the north coast of Scotland. A broken ship in a broken fleet, sir. A fleet broken by British courage and British seamanship.

'No one has a higher respect for the monarchy than myself, but I've always thought that Queen Elizabeth's inscription on the Armada medal is an insult to our heritage. God may have blown with his wind, but Medina Sidonia had lost the battle before the wind arrived. Drake defeated the Spaniards, Sir Marcus. Francis

Drake and the British Navy.' He paused to let the sentiment sink in.

'As for that twaddle about the *Veronica* being wrecked, I can only regard it with contempt. Lord Hector Cameron, who was the laird at the time, lied to whitewash himself, and my researches tell a very different story. I've visited the area on several occasions. I've talked to the people, consulted parish records and checked local tradition. I know what happened, and if James Clyde locates that galleon, it will be because I told him where to look.' It had been decided to keep the news of the epidemic secret and Fetherstone was unaware of what had actually been located on the peninsula.

'When the galleon was first spotted she was drifting with sails furled, and the boarding party discovered that, apart from the usual swarms of rats and cockroaches, there was only one living creature on her. Valdes himself. All the rest of her complement had been committed to the deep, as the service puts it.

'Valdes was taken ashore and kindly treated for a while. Then he was murdered and buried in a deserted stretch of marshland, still known as the Field of Ugliness. After the burial, which was conducted without benefit of clergy, the galleon was scuttled.

'Why, Sir Marcus?' There was a thud as the admiral's fist hammered his desk to emphasize the question. 'Why should Lord Hector Cameron, a Catholic with no love of the Protestant English, have killed his guest who was a co-religionist? Why should Valdes have been deprived of the Last Rites, and interred in unconsecrated ground? Why should the place of burial been given such an unsavoury name?

'Finally, and this is the moot point . . . why should a poverty-stricken highland chieftain and his clansmen scuttle a valuable vessel?'

'I'm hoping that you can tell me, Admiral Fetherstone.' Mark had started to form a theory and his excitement was mounting. Though the facts suggested that nuclear radiation had been involved, they could be misleading, and another possibility occurred to him – a worse one. If it was true, James Clyde had had good reason to ask for his help and Tania's study of the magazine article had solved the question.

Clyde's men didn't find a galleon – they found a coffin.

# Eight

Sunlight, silver sands and a sea as blue as the Mediterranean. Little white clouds soaring over the mountains which were gay with heather and willowherb. Sheep grazing on the fells and the murmur of trout streams. A lovely, peaceful coast, Mark had thought in the car taking him from Glasgow airport to Liskerg. Just the place for a holiday – a place to relax.

But he didn't think so now. Standing in the laboratory of Liskerg Cottage Hospital with the familiar smells of antiseptic and decay he had experienced since his student days, he knew that there was no time for relaxation or peace. He was on the perimeter of a battlefield.

Clyde's private army had been disbanded and arrested, but the barriers remained and regular forces guarded them. The peninsula was still a public danger and apart from volunteers with protective masks and clothing, nobody had entered it.

'Over two hundred corpses have been counted already and that is one of them.' There were three people in the room. Mark himself, Emily Repton and William Lawrence, who was speaking. 'A few survivors may be hiding out in the mountains, but I think it unlikely. In my opinion the entire population has been annihilated.'

'Then I'm afraid we must hope you're correct, Bill.' Mark was a doctor, his job was to preserve life, but he knew that death had been the only salvation for the thing displayed on a trestle-table. A thing that had been as lethal as the atomic weapons James Clyde tried to perfect. Flame-throwers had removed much of the evidence, but it could still be recognized as the body of a man – a sort of man.

'We have not dismantled either of the bombs yet, Sir Marcus. That would be too risky till special equipment is flown in.' Emily Repton was a cripple with one leg longer than the other and a pronounced spinal curvature. 'But none of the corpses show signs of radiation. Strange, though inconclusive. Under certain conditions the activity is short-lived.

'Yes, a radiation victim could pass on his physical symptoms to others, but as for the mental disturbances? The homicidal tendencies and so forth . . .' Mark had asked two questions and she hesitated over the second. 'I suppose the answer is *possibly*.

'During the Americans' early atomic tests in the Pacific, various species of wildlife completely changed their habits and could be described as insane. Turtles lost their sense of direction and walked away from the sea to die. Birds ceased to build nests and dug burrows like rabbits. I think that some experiments at Rushton Park produced similar results, but they were abandoned shortly before I took over there and the records are unavailable.'

'Thank you.' Mark was staring down at the charred face on the table, and he remembered the face of the living victim Weber had displayed on the film screen. The resemblance was clear enough and he considered how the outbreak had begun. A radiologist named Fred Brown with symptoms similar to those of influenza. Sore throat – shivering – a slight temperature and general malaise. That did not tie up with the little Mark knew about nuclear contamination and he was beginning to feel more and more certain that Admiral Fetherstone had provided a key to the solution.

'Hans Weber and the others have no idea what went wrong, Mark.' Lawrence interrupted his thoughts. 'Nor had Clyde, but the fact that he called you to the conference implies that he considered an organic factor might be involved. Do you think that likely?'

'I believe there may have been a combination of both organic and inorganic factors, Bill. After all, microorganisms are subject to radiation attack as well as the higher animals. Brown was working with dangerous substances in the laboratory. He could have handled something equally dangerous outside the lab and the union of the two produced that.' Mark nodded at the table and then glanced towards the window.

'In any case those chaps may have something interesting to show us.' A lorry had drawn up and Mark pondered his theory while he watched three soldiers sliding an object on to a trolley. He thought of the longevity of microbes. Germs producing spores that could lie dormant for centuries till favourable conditions revived them in more virulent forms. Forms which might become far, far more virulent under the stimulus of radiation. He thought of the potato blight which had twice ravaged Ireland. He thought of immunity. Carriers living contentedly with their disease and spreading it to all who came in close contact with them.

'Yes, something very interesting,' he repeated, trying to sound unemotional, though he'd never been more worried. As Professor Repton had said, radiation effects might be short-lived, but the enemy he feared was virtually immortal.

'Over there please.' The door had opened and the soldiers were wheeling their load into the room. A long, leaden box encrusted with mud from the Field of Ugliness.

'Thanks.' One of the men had handed Mark a screwdriver and he waited for them to withdraw before bending over the container. A coffin which Clyde's salvage team had unsealed and then reburied. Spades had scraped some of the grime from its lid and a Latin inscription was clear to the naked eye. Mark read it and then turned to Lawrence and Emily Repton.

'My witness for the prosecution,' he said. 'Don Francesco Valdes, the commander of a Spanish naval unit.' In spite of his anxiety, a pompous joke seemed appropriate. 'A witness who died a long time ago, but he may have started the ball rolling.'

'The *Santa Veronica* was found in a bay a few miles from here and there was only one man aboard her; the captain.' Mark wore a mask impregnated with antiseptic and he had told Lawrence and Professor Repton to stand back from the trolley. 'The supposition is that Valdes was well treated for a while. Then murdered and buried in unconsecrated ground, and the ship scuttled.

'Though no definite evidence is available I can hazard a guess why. The crew died of disease, and though Valdes was also a victim of the complaint he remained in good health. He had learned to live with his illness.'

The coffin lid had been fixed back into position by modern screws. They turned easily, though Mark was hampered by protective gloves, and while he worked he tried to explain his suspicions. Longevity and immunity. Spore-producing organisms and the animal system adapting itself to the presence of a hostile parasite.

'A person suffers from disease, Bill; typhoid or diphtheria for example. The invasion flourishes for a while, but the patient recovers because certain protective substances in his system – antitoxins, antibodies – control it. Control, but not destroy, however. The germs are still active, and though the victim regains normal health, he is ...'

'A carrier.' Only two screws remained in position and Lawrence was dragging at a cigarette to steady his nerves. 'Wasn't there a classic case in the States once? A woman who moved from job to job and deliberately infected several people?'

'Quite correct, Bill. They called her Typhoid Mary.' Mark was releasing the last screw and he shared Lawrence's dread. Though not because Francesco Valdes might have been a deliberate carrier. Valdes had died long ago. He couldn't breathe into his face or reach out to claw at his flesh and contaminate him. But the body might – just might – house needle-sharp spores which had been activated by air and moisture when the coffin was re-opened. Spores that a radiologist had handled. If so, there really were demons on the rampage. Tiny, mutated monsters capable of drifting through air and floating on water.

Monsters which only heat could kill. The last screw was loose and Mark glanced at the body on the trestle before withdrawing it. James Clyde had known that fire was a safeguard and that was why flame-throwers were used. But had he realized it was merely a temporary protection? Had he committed suicide because he knew that defeat was inevitable?

Fire killed, moisture and fresh air revived, and Mark thought of the pleasant trout streams he had passed on the way to Liskerg. If his fears were correct, the victims on the peninsula would soon have company. The real epidemic was about to begin.

But there was no time for conjecture. The contents of the coffin had to be examined and he pulled out the remaining screw and tilted the heavy lid aside. It fell to the floor with a dull thud and Mark looked at the Spanish sea captain.

Don Francesco Valdes had been buried in 1588, but he was far better preserved than his neighbour on the trestle-table. Fire had wasted the present-day corpse. Lead had screened Valdes from decay, and one glance told Mark everything – almost everything. Even the wooden spike protruding from the rib-cage was explained. Not an ordinary stake; a rather beautiful crucifix, before mutilation. Christ's feet and the base of his cross had been whittled into a point and hammered through the Spaniard's heart.

'I don't know if the Scots thought Valdes was a vampire.' Mark's gloved hands reached out to check the conclusive evidence. 'But they did consider him to be a bringer of disaster.'

'How right they were, and how wrong I was about immunity. This poor devil was not immune to the disease. He was merely the last man on the galleon to be infected and the symptoms did not appear till he came ashore.'

'Yes, that's that.' Mark's fingers probed into the mummified groin while he spoke. The proof was there. The swellings called buboes were present. He could feel them and see them, and he knew he was looking at the big one. The most lethal one – the most repulsive one – the worst killer in history. A scourge that had swept across the globe time and time again. Which had decimated populations almost over night and changed the economic structures of continents.

Which had also created superstition, mania and persecution – so the crucifix was explained. During one outbreak, people had danced naked in the streets till they dropped dead with exhaustion. They had flogged themselves in the streets to prepare for the torments of hell. They had coupled with strangers in the streets believing that sexual intercourse could cleanse them and pass on their agony to others.

A visitation from God, they'd called it. A sickness of the soil, because the rats and mice crawled out of the earth to die. They had considered that cats – the familiars of witches – were responsible and destroyed them, allowing the rodents to multiply. Then they had looked for human scapegoats and decided who the culprits were. The well-poisoners – the Jews – and the pogroms began. More than forty thousand Jews had been killed in Burgundy alone. Rabbis crucified head-down like Saint Peter. Children flung into fires because their parents refused to accept Christian baptism.

'There is no doubt whatsoever.' Mark's examination was finished and he straightened from the coffin. 'Give me a hand to replace the lid, Bill, and once again take my advice and relax.' To prove his confidence he removed a glove and stroked the face of the dead Armada captain.

'This chap is quite innocent. He only suffered from bubonic plague.'

'Plague – bubonic plague.' Mark had spoken almost cheerfully. Emily Repton had just received a telephone call and her sallow features registered relief, but Lawrence felt stunned by the statement. Plague – the very word was horrifying, and he thought of its other names. The Black Death, the Dark Maiden, the Ring of Roses.

'What the hell are you looking so cheerful about?' He ignored Mark's request to help him reseal the coffin and drew back even further from the trolley. 'I'm not a doctor, but I know a little about plague epidemics. I know how they operate.'

Lawrence was a hypochondriac. He had a comprehensive medical encyclopedia in his Whitehall flat and had read about the plague cycle. The bacilli living in the bloodstream of the rat flea, *xenopsylla cheopis*, which experiences no ill-effects from their presence. But the flea bites its host; the rat is infected, leaves its hole, and dies. After a period of between two to four days, depending on climatic conditions, the flea deserts the rat's carcass and attaches itself to man and other animals. The epidemic has begun.

'Plague practically wiped out Alexandria and Byzantium and Carthage, Mark. During the Black Death over a quarter of the entire population of Europe died. Yet, you say that that – that man, *only* suffered from it. If natural plague can cause such massive destruction what could a strain strengthened by radiation do?'

'A great deal, Colonel.' Emily Repton obviously shared Mark's relief. 'An outbreak of mutated *bacillus pestis* is a terrifying prospect. Nobody knows that better than myself, because part of our work at Rushton Park is concerned with biological warfare.

'But, in this instance, I think the prospect can be discounted. Am I right, Sir Marcus?'

'Perfectly right.' Though Mark disapproved of the work she'd

mentioned and heard that Professor Repton was an unpleasant woman who bullied her staff, he warmed towards her as she
limped over to help him raise the heavy lid. 'My worry was that
Valdes suffered from a less dramatic illness than plague; maybe
influenza.'

'Flu?' Lawrence was starting to believe that both his companions had lost their wits. 'That's nothing compared to bubonic
plague . . . a mere flea bite.'

'An unfortunate comparison, Bill. Plague is transmitted by flea
bites.' Mark took a last glance at the coffin's occupant before the
lid slid back into position. 'But, though the plague bacilli, both
bubonic and pneumonic are usually more lethal than flu they have
a weakness – an Achilles' heel.

'They do not produce spores and are short lived. Like the fleas
which carry them, they need fresh blood for nourishment. The
organisms which attacked Valdes and his crew died with their
victims.' Mark made a calculation. 'They died 388 years ago, and
Valdes is the man we have to think about.'

'Though not to worry about, in my view, Sir Marcus.' Emily
Repton stared at the body on the trestle-table. 'Specimens must
naturally be sent to Rushton Park for thorough examination, and
you will probably want others delivered to St Bede's hospital.
There are no facilities available here.

'Clyde's bombs will be rendered harmless as soon as we have
the equipment, and that should be the end of our worries. The
telephone call I received stated that all the corpses, so far located,
are now free of radiation which the man, Frederick Brown, almost
certainly picked up and spread around the peninsula.

'An unfortunate occurrence which killed a large number of people, but it's over now.' She straightened her misshapen spine and
smiled at Lawrence. 'A flash in the pan, Colonel.

'Or, as you put it – a flea bite.'

'Just a touch of flu, but damn this bloody cough.' Dr Allan Carlin
cursed loudly as he walked over the Cornish moors towards the
sea. 'Damn my chest and my throat and my blasted shakes.' It was
a hot day, but though Carlin was sweating freely he shivered with

cold. 'Must be flu, but where the hell did I pick it up? Who could have given it to me?'

A good question, because Carlin came into contact with very few people. Since retirement he had become a recluse with no close friends and hardly any acquaintances. He ordered his groceries and other supplies by telephone, and they were usually left in the porch of his cottage when he was out. He had little contact with his neighbours, and when the vicar had paid a call and said he should take an interest in communal affairs, he'd given the sanctimonious fool a piece of his mind.

An ill-tempered, solitary individual, Allan Carlin, but not a lonely one. He had his books and his radio, his television and his sketching. He had a Siamese cat and he found himself excellent company. Till yesterday his only correspondence had concerned business, and that was the way he liked it. He didn't want to be reminded of the past, and he didn't need his fellow men. He kept himself to himself, so from whom had he caught the bug, and who had sent him that ridiculous message?

'A loving friend from Rushton Park . . . a friend of Brown's.' That was how the note had been signed and it didn't make sense. He'd made no friends at the research establishment and he and Frederick Brown had had only one thing in common; a blunder. An unfortunate mishap, which had cost them their jobs and might have caused a woman's death. All most unfortunate.

Damn the letter-writer – damn this flu. Carlin cursed again, but not aloud. He'd been racked by a fit of coughing which brought him to a halt and made him abandon his project to paint a watercolour of the Green Cormorant Cove.

Flu – a nasty bout, and he'd better do something about it. He turned reluctantly and started to walk away from the sea, though not towards the village. He was a doctor of science, but he had as much medical knowledge as young Egerton, the local G.P. Egerton would prescribe antibiotics and he distrusted them. He had reason to – good reason.

Sweating was the only safe way to cure influenza. Whisky and aspirin – plenty of whisky. A really hot mustard-bath and rest. He'd dose himself with Scotch, go to bed with an electric blanket under the sheet and be as right as rain in the morning.

Bed! The prospect was attractive, but the letter still troubled Allan Carlin as he hurried home as fast as his aching legs could carry him. A brief note enclosed in a peculiar envelope. The material was some kind of thin, waterproof plastic, though the card inside was as thick and spongy as blotting paper.

He somehow felt that the writing was familiar to him, but he couldn't place its author. He didn't want to, because the message revived bad memories. 'A short line to commemorate our happy associations at Rushton. Trust you haven't forgotten them, Allan, and if you have, don't worry. You and dear Fred Brown will be swapping reminiscences very shortly.'

Just that, followed by the 'loving friend' signature. Nonsense – malicious, lying nonsense. His spell at Rushton Park had not been happy and he hadn't liked Fred Brown; not one little bit. Brown was an incompetent, over-sexed oaf and mainly responsible for what had happened. If bloody Fred Brown called to swap old memories he'd have the door slammed in his face.

Damn Brown . . . damn the letter-writer. Damn this bloody chill, though that was nothing to worry about. A sore throat, a congested chest, a bit of a temperature and the shivers. Nothing that whisky, aspirin and a good, long sweat on the electric blanket wouldn't cure.

A touch of flu.

# Nine

'Interesting, but inconclusive.' A chair creaked as fat John Forest, editor of the London *Daily Globe*, eased his vast bulk into a more comfortable position. 'Mark went into no more detail, Tania?' Forest had explained his visit as soon as he arrived at the Levins' house. He was a newspaper man – he wanted news.

'No, John.' Tania had been friendly with Forest for a long time and, though she enjoyed his company, she distrusted him completely. In normal circumstances, she would never have confided in him, but for the present his hands were tied. He had shown her

a photostated letter from the Ministry of Internal Security which
had been issued to all newspapers. An order prohibiting any men-
tion of the situation until an official statement was released. There
was no harm in talking to Forest and she had welcomed his visit.
Mark's phone call from Liskerg had been brief and she wanted
news herself. 'Now you tell me what you know, John.'

'Of course I will, my dear, and thank you very – very much. You
are kindness personified . . . the soul of hospitality.' The fat man
had a sweet tooth and he beamed at the laden tray she placed on
a table at his side. 'Chocolate éclairs, chocolate biscuits and a glass
of cherry brandy.

'Delicious. So, what shall I sample first?' He picked up an éclair,
ate half in a single bite and washed it back with a sip of the brandy.

'You have been frank with me and, naturally, I'll reciprocate,
though Mark will have probably told you as much as I can.' He finished the éclair and drank again. 'We're snoopers – that's our job
– and the paper always has two chaps stationed at London airport to
note the arrival and departure of V.I.P.s. Jaimie Clyde does not, or
rather *did* not, answer that description in the technical sense of the
term, but he had definite news value and one of our men followed
his car to the house near Strenton.' Forest reached for a biscuit.

'A laudable piece of diligence, though it turned out to be
unnecessary, because Sam Kahn, my boss, was also invited to the
conference. That meeting of the minds which was interrupted so
tragically.

'Clyde cut his throat and the story was completed by one of his
henchmen. A kraut who now calls himself Hans Weber, though
his original name is more appropriate: Willi Hardt. A hard fellow
who was convicted of crimes against humanity after the war and
served thirteen years in a West German prison.

'Weber-Hardt described the situation in Scotland. A rural
population struck by radiation leakage which produced spectacular results; physical deformities and homicidal urges. The area
cordoned off on Clyde's orders and the surviving inhabitants
murdered to check the outbreak. A sad story which may not have
ended.' Forest sighed; a sound like the clearing of a blocked drain.

'Clyde's retainers have been rounded up and isolated in an ex-

R.A.F. camp and the army are still guarding the cordons. And yet Mark advised you not to worry, Tania. Could it have been a white lie to lull your fears?'

'Mark doesn't lie to me, John.' Tania spoke sharply, but she suspected Forest might be right, because Mark had seemed hesitant and deliberately vague on the telephone. 'He said that the danger was probably over, though specialized tests would be needed for full confirmation.'

'Tests which will be carried out at St Bede's Hospital and Rushton Park, I presume.' Forest emptied his glass, rolling the liqueur around his mouth before swallowing it. 'Rushton Park is a most versatile establishment. They deal in everything from Polaris warheads to cures for the common cold.

'A secretive establishment, too. I got short shrift when I was last there in . . .' He paused to concentrate. 'Four, five, six years ago? No, I can't recall the date. The old memory cells decay rapidly and booze speeds up the process.' He grimaced at the glass.

'Another unfortunate mishap though, and the authorities tried to hush it up as they are doing in the present instance.' Forest was speaking to himself as much as to Tania and he leaned forward; his great bloated belly thrusting against bolster-like thighs.

'What did happen at Rushton? Three people were involved – that I can remember. One man was called Brown and the other Carlin, but who was the third? The girl who vanished? Ann – Anna – Anita? Her Christian name was something like that, but the surname escapes me, and what does it matter? Experiments must often go wrong and there can't be a connection with the Clyde business. Not after all those years.'

'Then why are you considering the possibility, John?' Tania refilled his glass. 'What did go wrong at Rushton Park?'

'I never knew for sure, my dear, but there was a similarity between the two instances and it's coming back.' He paused again. 'Yes, the girl was called Annabel something-or-other and she behaved rather like those people in Scotland.

'She went potty and smashed things.'

Changeable weather is a postman's worst enemy, Harry Lloyd

thought, parking his van at the side of the lane and climbing out. It had been chilly before he went to work and his wife had told him to put on a thick vest. But, halfway through his round the wind had dropped and the atmosphere became hot and humid. He was sweating freely and the vest clung to his body like an elastic bandage.

Not to grumble, however. Merrytor Cottage was his final call and in a few minutes he'd be downing two pints of bitter beer in the cool bar of his local. The first glass would be raised in honour of a former employer. Ernest Marples, the Postmaster General who'd examined his men's lot personally; donning the peaked cap and heavy uniform and discovering what torture they were in the heat.

Ernie had been the best P.M.G. of them all, in Lloyd's opinion, though there were still many ways to improve a postman's lot. More pay, shorter hours and the abolition of formal clothing. Even in midsummer one had to wear a regulation jacket for identification purposes, and it was unnecessary and unfair. The police got away with shirts and badges – why not postmen?

It was also unfair that he should have had to come such a long way for nothing – or virtually nothing. Merrytor Cottage was right off the beaten track, there was no drive leading to it and he had to climb a stile and cross a field to make his deliveries. People like Dr Carlin should have collection boxes by the roadside, same as they did in the States.

Not that Carlin gave him much work. Lloyd clambered over the stile and set off along the narrow footpath. The old sod hardly received any mail, though there had been that strange letter last Tuesday. Carlin was in the garden when Lloyd arrived, and as usual he made no offer of a cup of tea or a bottle of beer. Just a gruff, 'Thank you, Postman,' and a nod of dismissal.

Unsociable old brute. A hermit who spent most of the day wandering about the moors and shunned his neighbours – was bloody rude to them, in fact. Shortly after he moved into the cottage the vicar had paid a friendly call and Carlin made his attitude clear.

'I intend to take no interest in local affairs, Padre,' he had said, scowling from the doorway. 'Nor do I require spiritual instruction. I own a Bible and am perfectly capable of consulting the word of God when the need arises.'

Yes, a rum cove. No car, no phone – not even a dog for company and protection, though the cottage was isolated. Stupid, as well as rude and unsociable. There were such things as heart attacks and a lot of bad characters around. Gipsies and drugged hippies and escaped criminals on the run. If Carlin had an illness or was beaten up, he couldn't call for help. If he died, it might be days – weeks – before his body was discovered.

Might Carlin be a wanted criminal himself? Harry Lloyd was an avid reader of thrillers and the more lurid Sunday newspapers, and the possibility had frequently occurred to him. Could fear of recognition explain his behaviour? Certainly that last letter suggested he had an enemy or a creditor or someone he hated. After Lloyd started to walk back to his van, he'd heard a curse and swung round. The envelope had been opened and its contents didn't please Carlin. His tanned face was as red as a boiled lobster and he was tearing a piece of paper into shreds. A scene that made Lloyd think of a Sherlock Holmes story; 'The Dancing Men', or 'The Boscombe Valley Tragedy'? He couldn't remember which, but there'd been a similar scene in one of them.

A rum cove and a rum communication. Lloyd would have liked to know what the communication was, but there'd be no fun and games today. The letter in his hand could only irritate people, and he'd delivered six identical envelopes during the morning. Circulars from 'The Householder's Easi-Loan Fellowship', most of which would be thrown away unopened.

Rightly thrown away. The senders were con-men, who obtained names and addresses from the rates list, and made thorough nuisances of themselves to everyone. They wasted time and energy and paper. Commodities the world needed desperately and all such circulars should be banned.

'Hello, Puss.' Allan Carlin's sole companion; an undersized Siamese cat, was crouched beside the path and Lloyd stooped to stroke it. A friendly gesture, which was not appreciated. The animal snarled at him, and arched its back. Another unsociable brute,

and an ugly one. More like a rodent or a hedgehog than a cat in
Lloyd's view. Give him a decent English tabby, any time.

Carlin was not in the garden and the cottage door was open.
An unusual occurrence which pleased Lloyd, because he'd often
wanted to have a look inside. He read Dickens, as well as thrillers and newspapers, and believed that possessions told tales about
their owners. It was hardly likely that the sitting-room contained
anything as dramatic as Miss Haversham's decayed wedding-cake
in *Great Expectations*, but there might be something to give him a
clue to the doctor's past; photographs, maybe.

'Good morning to you, Dr Carlin.' He grinned widely, though
he felt pretty certain his grin wouldn't raise any answering smile of
welcome. No beer, or tea, nor an invitation to sit down and have a
chat.

'A damned hot morning and I'm . . .' Lloyd was about to say *fair
parched* in the unlikely hope of hospitality, but he broke off and
gasped. There was no sign of Carlin and surprise and fear stifled
his words.

The same fear that Mary Alison and the helicopter crew had
experienced, and it was not produced by the things he saw, though
they were disturbing enough. Pictures slashed and torn from their
frames, – the overturned furniture on the floor – the broken glass
and crockery on the floor – the Victorian cavalry sabre on the
floor. A sharp sword – the weapon he needed.

The cottage looked as though it had been ransacked, but the
destruction did not make Harry Lloyd's mouth droop open and
send him dashing forward to pick up the sabre. He was not alone,
and a sound had caused his shock and consternation. A threatening sound – an unexpected one.

To Lloyd's certain knowledge, Dr Allan Carlin did not keep pigs.

## Ten

'You're still tired.' Tania eyed Mark with concern. He had arrived
home three hours ago, spent two of them in bed, and now
intended to start work at the hospital. 'Can't it wait till tomorrow,

or couldn't someone else take over from you?'

'You're probably right on both counts darling, but I want to make those tests now, and nobody is going to take my place. I am a conceited man with an inquisitive mind.' Though he was tired, Mark knew that he couldn't sleep till the questions had been answered.

'I'm almost certain that the captain and crew of the Spanish galleon suffered from plague,' he said. 'A virulent, but short-lived complaint which could hardly have been responsible for the current tragedies. Emily Repton is equally certain that they were caused by a release of radiation which has since died out.

'I think she's correct, but we must have confirmation that no bacillus, or virus, or any other form of microorganism was involved. That's why I've arranged to pick up Edgar Godspel at eight o'clock.' Mark glanced at his watch. 'Godspel may be a bore, but he's a first-class analyst.

'The tests shouldn't take too long. St Bede's has a well-equipped lab and specimens have already been delivered there.'

'Some specimens to St Bede's – others to Rushton Park.' Tania remembered what John Forest had told her. *Polaris warheads to cures for the common cold.* 'Are germ warfare experiments conducted at Rushton, Mark?'

'Just about every kind of experiment is conducted there. Rushton Park is probably the largest and most comprehensive research establishment in Europe. Excluding Mother Russia, of course.' Mark smiled mockingly. Tania had been a Soviet citizen before their marriage and she still retained her patriotism. 'Your people build everything bigger and better and more efficiently than the rest of the world, Or so I've read in *Pravda*.'

'Where security is concerned they are certainly more efficient than the English, Mark.' Tania grinned back at him. She had been about to repeat Forest's half recalled story, but there was no point. Though the incident was an intriguing mystery, it had happened long ago and could have no bearing on modern events.

'If Sir James Clyde was Russian he'd have been rumbled from the start.' Tania spoke with pride. 'Rumbled and dealt with before he could cause any trouble.'

'I'm sure that's true. The K.G.B. would have stood the poor, crazy bastard against a wall or packed him off to Siberia.' Though he was preoccupied, Mark considered the different viewpoints of democracy and totalitarianism and the problem of malevolent genius. Attila and Tamburlaine, Hitler and Stalin . . . all the dynamic characters who had created ruin and misery. Jaimie Clyde too, in a smaller way. Would it have been better if they had been killed at birth, or condemned to execution squads and madhouses? Maybe, but what about the others – the benevolent ones, who brought joy and knowledge? Humanity rarely distinguishes good from evil till it is too late, and distrusts anything unusual. Shakespeare and Beethoven and the Buddha might also have been condemned.

An unanswerable, age-old problem. But there was a present day question which could be answered, and he had the means to do so. Scientific instruments and dead tissue. Liver, kidneys, heart, lungs and other organs. The stock-in-trade of a cats'-meat merchant, but in this case it was human tissue. The remains of a man killed by bullets and disfigured by fire.

A man who would tell him that the epidemic was at an end. That it had been caused by a radiation leakage which had died out. That the worry was over and his tests at the hospital would be purely academic.

Mark was confident about that, but then he'd always been confident. Even in Warsaw and Belsen and Ruhleben he had felt sure of survival. Now he was rich and successful and an internationally recognized authority. He had been anxious at the beginning, but his fears were groundless. Francesco Valdes had suffered from plague and it was a coincidence that the current victims shared his lion-faced features. Atomic pollution was the sole cause and no micro-organism had been responsible. In an hour or two he'd be proved right. His knowledge and qualifications guaranteed that. He was a Knight Companion of the Bath, a Fellow of the Royal Society, and a Nobel Prize winner, and he knew his job. The danger was over and he must – must – must be right, he reassured himself.

More fool he.

The sun was going down and the petrol tank was empty. But Harry Lloyd didn't know the exact time, or how far he had travelled before the engine faltered and coughed to a halt. His watch had been broken during the fight in the cottage. He was ill and dazed and he couldn't concentrate.

Even the details of the struggle were vague now, though he remembered lunging out with the sword before a blow knocked him senseless. A fortunate lunge which saved him. When consciousness returned he saw that the assailant was lying sideways on the floor; the curved sabre blade protruding from his back.

Or *its* back. Lloyd had no idea who or what had attacked him, though it wasn't Carlin who emerged from the bedroom. The doctor was thin and frail and elderly. The figure that rushed at him had been bloated – almost deformed – and as strong as a bull. He didn't know why he hadn't examined the body before staggering out of the cottage. He didn't know why he hadn't driven to the police station after he reached the van. Harry Lloyd knew very little.

Shock perhaps – fear and the effects of concussion. An urge to flee from the terror behind him. To drive – drive – drive, and he'd certainly done that. The tank had been almost full when he reached Merrytor Cottage and he'd travelled a long distance. Main roads and minor roads and a stretch of motorway. Through towns and villages and open country. No plan, no route, no destination. Just the blind compulsion to chalk up the miles and escape.

But was it possible that he hadn't escaped? That the sword had missed a vital organ, and the creature in the cottage was not dead? That it had followed him across the field and shared his journey? Unlikely, but he couldn't be sure. He was too tired to concentrate. More tired and weak than he'd ever been.

Also, more terrified. Had it only been the springs creaking when he crossed that bridge? Had the exhaust echoed under the railway arch? Was it a tyre whine he had heard on the motorway? Or, had something opened the rear door and climbed into the luggage compartment?

A horrible possibility, but it would be suicidal to slide back the panel behind him and make sure. Though he was ill and had been beaten insensible – though the graze on his cheek was throbbing painfully, he still had a few wits left and he wasn't insane. Cunning was needed – cunning and deception. He'd get out, pretend to examine the engine and then run . . . run for his life.

Harry Lloyd's plan almost succeeded. He released the bonnet catch, opened the driving-seat door and prepared to dash towards the thicket of trees which lay ahead. His right foot was on the ground when he saw the reflection in the wing-mirror and screamed.

Though he had no personal reason to be frightened. The sword thrust had been lethal. Nobody had followed him from Carlin's cottage and entered the van. Apart from two crows perched on a telegraph pole the road was deserted and he was quite alone.

The thing that frightened him was his own face.

## Eleven

'As I expected.' There were five microscopes on the laboratory bench and Mark was craning over the first of them. Edgar Godspel had prepared an excellent slide and the picture was rather beautiful. A universe of dead human cells stained purple by an alkaline dye which made them visible.

But there were also non-human cells present. Small oval capsules which confirmed Mark's snap diagnosis at Liskerg. The enemies that had wiped out the crew of an Armada galleon and died with their victims. 'That's plague all right and we can ignore the Spaniards, Doctor. There is naturally no sign of spore productions.'

'None to be seen so far.' Godspel peered through the second eyepiece. Mark had explained the situation to him during the drive to the hospital and the little man was tense and excited. 'But can anyone say for certain that plague never sporifies? What about that case in Norfolk? An archaeologist excavating a graveyard which dated from the Black Death. He died mysteriously and the symptoms were similar to bubonic plague.'

'Only similar, and there was no scientific proof to support the theory. The newspapers exaggerated the facts, and food poisoning was the more probable cause of his illness.' Mark straightened from the microscope and frowned. 'You're right about the Black Death, of course. That will always remain a mystery and might have been due to an unusual strain – a natural variation of the species.

'There's nothing unusual about those chaps, though. They're perfectly normal plague bacilli, so let's forget Valdes and concentrate on the modern exhibits.' He turned to the second instrument and studied the blood corpuscles of a Scottish hill farmer.

'We appear to be wasting our time, Doctor, and please God we continue to do so.' Mark could see signs of deformity which might have been caused by radiation, though no suggestion of actual disease. Reassuring, but indefinite. Heat had destroyed much of the evidence and there were many more specimens to examine.

Heart – negative. Liver and kidneys – also negative. Mark moved along the row of instruments. Each picture showed the same deformities and two of them suggested that the man had been a heavy spirit-drinker. But nothing else – nothing to concern Godspel or himself – nothing of value.

Lung tissue and . . . The image was indistinct and he turned the fine adjustment knob. Yes . . . yes . . . yes. The focus improved; he did see something significant at last. A cluster of minute, cross-shaped objects.

'A virus?' Godspel had sensed his excitement and joined him at the microscope. 'Just for a moment, I thought I saw one of them move.'

'So did I, Doctor, though we must be wrong. The alkaline dye is bound to have killed them. But let's try a hanging droplet system instead of the stain and have a look at Mr Big – the First Fiddle.' Mark was referring to the pituitary gland. 'If he was infected, a lot of questions are answered.'

Mark stood back from the eyepiece and watched Godspel prepare the equipment. While he waited, he considered the phenomenon of longevity, as he had done at Liskerg. Wheat grains recovered from the coffin of an Egyptian Pharaoh, germinating. Grass seeds sprouting after being buried under a stone slab for four hundred years.

He also considered the function of the pituitary. A small organ, but an important one; the Leader of the Orchestra, which governed the entire human system. If the leader played a wrong note, his fellow musicians followed suit and a thousand abnormalities could be created.

'Good.' Godspel had beckoned to him and he hurried over to the instrument. 'Yes, very good – excellent in fact.' Refracted light and liquid made the specimen visible and he could see more of the cruciform objects floating on a drop of distilled water. And one of them was definitely moving. He saw the base and arms of the cross break away from the headpiece and start to bulge. The parasite had survived the death of its host. Moisture was reviving the dormant spores and they were reproducing themselves.

'Well, Edgar,' Mark said. Excitement and worry brought out the first name automatically. He and Godspel were not merely colleagues. They were soldiers fighting an enemy – comrades sharing a front-line dug-out. 'Your opinion is as good as mine, so what do you think it is? A natural variation?'

'How can either of us know at this stage, Sir Marcus?' Godspel was too tense to notice the familiarity. 'But, as you've asked for my opinion, I'll hazard one.

'I think that James Clyde may have been trying to produce more than an atomic bomb.' His eye remained glued to the lens and his face was ashen.

'My guess – hunch – suspicion, is that those things are man-made: mutated flu.'

He was still terrified, but he mustn't panic. The threat remained, he had to keep his wits about him. He was alone at the moment though; Harry Lloyd was sure of that.

Nobody had followed him across the field to the van and the grunting, slavering creature in Carlin's cottage was dead. The sword blow really had been a lucky one which penetrated the heart. The man, woman, or animal – whatever the being was – had died and it couldn't frighten him any more. Nor could the reflection in the wing-mirror frighten him, and there would be no other reflections. He'd picked up a stone from the roadside and broken the mirrors; all three of them. He'd also broken the windscreen and the windows and the dashboard, and hammered dents in the bodywork, though he didn't know why. He just wanted to break things – glass and plastic and metal. Flesh and blood too, if he got his hands on them, and soon – very soon.

The road in front of him sloped steeply down towards a bend, and though Lloyd couldn't see what was coming up the hill, he could hear it. A distant, innocent sound at the moment, but he recognized what it was. The same obscene grunting sound. The sound of pigs.

And he couldn't run away. Weights seemed to be fixed to his feet, though the rest of his body felt stronger than it had ever done and he was ready for the fight. Whatever form the enemy took, he had to fight it, because there was no escape.

Or was there? Reason returned briefly and Lloyd remembered the jerrican of petrol he'd picked up to deliver to Farmer Tomlin on his way back to the depot. An illegal act, but an act of friendship, and that four-gallon can might save him, if he hurried; really hurried.

Harry Lloyd stumbled round to the back of the van on his leaden feet, but as he opened the rear door and reached for the tin he realized he was too late.

The noise was much louder now. Hammering and pounding and grunting and there was no time to fill up the tank, turn round and drive away. The eyes of the creature had rounded the bend and were peering up at him. Bright, yellow eyes. The eyes of a Juggernaut; a god's chariot which crushed men and women beneath its wheels.

But, though he couldn't escape, he didn't really want to. He wanted to attack and destroy, and what was to stop him? Lloyd had served in the Western Desert during the war and he had once seen a German armoured car knocked out by a Molotov cocktail. A simple device, and there was one available. He opened the tin, stuffed his handkerchief tightly into its neck and waited for the petrol to soak the cloth. Then he stepped forward to fight his last battle.

The eyes of the Juggernaut were blinding. The grunting roar of its approach was quickening as the slope eased and the monster was only thirty yards away from him when Harry Lloyd struck a match and lit his homemade bomb. But the tin never left his grasp. Four gallons is a fair weight and before he could throw it, the petrol exploded.

'Blimey – cor blimey.' The crew of the heavily-laden lorry were quick-thinking men and they had done all they could when the sudden gout of fire roared in front of the bonnet and they saw the human figure writhing in the flames. The driver had slammed on the brakes and his mate snatched up a fire-extinguisher and jumped from the cab to render assistance.

Quick, but not quick enough. The fire was out, its victim was still alive, but only just. 'What's the poor bleeder trying to say – trying to tell us?' Both men were bent over the charred, broken body, but the driver's question would never be answered.

Harry Lloyd was not saying anything. He was grunting.

## Twelve

'A man-made mutant, Edgar?' Mark considered the possibility. 'Yes, that might be on the cards, and though you said you were only guessing, your tone was pretty confident. Any reason why?'

'No definite reason, Mark.' Godspel had also discarded formality. 'I'm just suspicious and bewildered. How could any natural aberration produce such extreme and rapid results? – the mental and physical changes you described to me. How can the spores withstand radiation, intense heat and alkaline dye?'

'We don't know that radiation was involved and the heat was not all that intense, though the changes were certainly dramatic.' Mark had told Godspel what he had seen on Clyde's projector screen. A poor, over-exposed photograph, but the subject was clear enough. A lion-faced creature crouched to spring at the cameraman before bullets and flames hurled it back.

'You could be right, Edgar. Every natural flu strain is transmitted by the breath and that did not happen in the present instance. If it had, Clyde and all his men would have been infected. I also

think we'll find that the units are too heavy to float in air. Actual
bodily contact is needed and the Ben Sagur people passed on their
complaint by a form of injection. They clawed and bit their victims so that the virus entered the bloodstream directly.'

That could account for the rapidity, Mark thought. Arteries and
veins carrying the parasite to the heart and lungs and glands. To
the pituitary gland – the First Fiddle who controlled everything.

'In any event your guess should be proved or disproved before
long, Edgar,' he said. Godspel was preparing cultures from the
things they had seen through the microscope, and Mark's eyes
kept flicking from him to the telephone. He had contacted William Lawrence at Liskerg and Lawrence would be calling back as
soon as he had checked his inquiries. But whatever Lawrence's
replies might be, Mark suspected that there was something more
important. Something he should remember. A chance remark – a
briefly made statement – a few casually spoken words – the necessary lead.

No, he couldn't remember those words and the phone was ringing at last. He snatched it up, announced himself and listened.

'I see, Bill.' Lawrence had sounded quite definite. 'Reassuring I
suppose, but we're not out of the woods yet – not by any means.'
He replaced the receiver and turned to Godspel.

'There was no radiation leak on the peninsula, Edgar. No biological experiments were carried out. There was no bacteriologist
among the men who have been arrested. The virus must be a natural variant unless . . . ?'

Unless? A notion had entered Mark's mind. With any luck the
culture saucers should soon be swarming with life, but it was not
life that interested him. Death might provide the answer.

'If we took a group of spores which did not germinate, carbon-
isotope tests should establish their date of origin.' He smiled at
Godspel's obvious bewilderment. 'You could be right about a man-
made mutation, Edgar.

'Though James Clyde didn't produce any biological weapons, a
lot of other people have.'

'You really are an oyster, my dear.' Kathleen Godspel leaned forward on the sofa. Shortly before Edgar and Mark left for Liskerg she had telephoned and asked Tania to keep her company. Tania had been glad of the invitation, but she was regretting it now. Her hostess had started to pump her and though confiding in John Forest was one thing – Mrs Godspel was quite another. Forest had to keep quiet because he was sworn to secrecy and the *Globe* would risk a massive fine if those orders were disobeyed. Kate Godspel was under no such prohibition, and women were usually more garrulous than men.

'Come on, Tania.' Like their husbands the two women had adopted Christian-name terms, and much more quickly. 'I'm agog for news, and why should the boys have all the fun?'

'I can't tell you anything, Kate, though I will say that *fun* is not the appropriate word.' Tania kept glancing at the photograph on the mantelpiece. She knew that she had seen that girl before, and not merely in a newspaper illustration. She had actually met her and spoken to her, though she couldn't imagine when, or where, or under what circumstances.

'Then let's say funny *peculiar* – not funny *ha-ha*.' Kate quoted from a once famous play. 'And it is peculiar and rather sinister. During our little soirée the other night, Mark receives a telephone call from someone named Colonel Lawrence and is rushed off in a police car. When I call you the following day, you say he has gone to the north of Scotland on business. Now he has returned and evoked Edgar's help. Why, Tania? Just what is that business?'

'I'm sorry, Kate.' Tania stood up. 'I promised Mark not to repeat anything he told me and I think it's time I went home.'

'Please don't go yet.' The woman's tone became pleading. 'We'll change the subject, but don't leave me. I'm lonely and worried – worried about Edgar.

'Poor Edgar. He could have been a successful man, but what is he now? An assistant – a checker of data for people like Mark. Also, a spasmodic drunkard and a habitual jester. Do you know why he drinks and makes those silly jokes?

'To conceal misery, my dear.' Tania had shaken her head and Kathleen Godspel's eyes flickered behind her thick spectacles. 'Edgar is the traditional clown who laughs to fight back tears, and all for the love of a lady. An old flame who went away, and he married me on the rebound. Soon he won't even have that poor substitute.

'Oh no, I'd never leave him. Not voluntarily, but I have no choice. I'm dying, you see.' She spoke unemotionally, as though discussing the weather or a minor news item. 'My body is riddled with cancer, though Edgar doesn't know it. He must never know till the terminal stage is reached. That's my secret, Tania, but there's no need to be sorry for me; only for Edgar. I don't regard life as a very valuable gift and I'd rather forget about the future.'

'As you wish, though I'm still extremely sorry.' Tania sat down and looked at the photograph. 'So, can we discuss the past? Who is that girl? I know I've met her somewhere, and you were going to tell me about her before Bill Lawrence telephoned the other night.'

'She was a poor, misguided bitch, Tania. A fool, who helped to ruin Edgar's life and her own, and you can't have met her. You saw her pictures in a newspaper or outside a police station. As I said, the story created quite a stir at the time – the autumn of 1970.'

'But it didn't create a stir in the Soviet Union.' Tania and Mark had been in Russia during that autumn: he attending a series of world health conferences in Moscow and Leningrad; she visiting her family. 'No, I'm sure I knew her personally, perhaps intimately, but I can't even remember her name.'

'Rather a romantic name, my dear. As romantic as her appearance.' There was more than a trace of envy in Kate's words. 'The title of a poem written by another Edgar. Maybe that's what aroused my Edgar's interest in the first place. Maybe he married me because my middle name is Anna.' She stroked her long black hair. 'This is my only physical attraction. But how does that verse start?' She frowned at the photograph and began to quote.

'Yes. "It was many and many a year ago in a kingdom by the sea, that a maiden lived whom you may know . . ."'

'I do know.' Tania interrupted her. On first settling in England she had imagined that the Anglo-Saxons lacked emotion till she read their lyric poets. Edgar Allan Poe was one of those poets and she took up the quotation.

'"That a maiden lived whom you may know by the name of Annabel Lee."'

# Thirteen

'Will nothing kill the blighters?' Mark straightened from a microscope for almost the hundredth time, and each picture had told the same story. The cultures Godspel had produced were still thriving. Dividing and multiplying faster than any organisms he had known. The fresh spores they released were sharper too, and he was sure that the mere touch of an infected person would be lethal. 'Nothing stop them?'

'Nothing we've used so far.' Edgar Godspel added a drop of clear liquid to one of the culture saucers. They had tried almost the full range of antibiotics and the tiny, cross-shaped creatures shrugged each of them aside. They appeared to flourish on the preparations. 'Nothing that wouldn't kill the host as well as the parasite.

'Fire, pure alcohol and acid does the trick, but one can hardly treat a patient with any of those remedies.' Godspel had examined the culture through a hand-lens and he looked up and nodded twice. First at a Bunsen burner, then at a half-bottle of whisky a porter had fetched from a nearby off-licence.

'And talking of alcohol, won't you join me in another drink? I can certainly use one.'

'No thanks, and please try to stay sober, Edgar.' Though Mark had only had a single Scotch, he saw that the bottle was three-quarters empty. 'I need your help.'

'You'll get it Mark. I'm sober enough.' Godspel poured himself another generous measure. 'I'm also frightened. These blighters, as you call them, are real devils. They must be man-made, and I've almost started to regard them as personal enemies.' He grimaced and looked at his watch. 'The night staff at Central Laboratories should be sending in their findings soon, but why did you ask for carbon-isotope tests? They can only establish the age of dead matter. Not living tissue, and these – these blighters are very much alive.'

'Like you, I have a hunch, Edgar.' Samples of inactive spores were being examined by other scientists and Mark was impatient to hear the results.

'Probably a worthless hunch, but it could be relevant. We're up against some form of mutated flu virus and I want to know when that mutation occurred.' Mark considered humanity's sadism and death-wish. Money, technical skills and countless, inoffensive animals sacrificed for the most hideous method of destruction – germ warfare.

'I'm beginning to share your view that the strain must be man-made, Edgar, and that implies an accidental leak from some laboratory. If we could establish the date of the mutation, the intelligence services might – just might – be able to find out what nation was working on those lines. To pin-point the place of origin and ask the people responsible for an antidote.

'There must be an antidote, Edgar; also a vaccine. No sane persons would attempt to create such monsters without working out defences against them. That would be suicidal.' Mark knew that his statements were vague and rambling, and he was speaking more to himself than to Godspel. He was also trying to reassure himself. Throughout his career he had learned a great deal about aberrations; man-made and natural. He knew as much as anyone about the behaviour of viruses, but the things swarming in the culture saucers were somehow uncanny. Like Edgar Godspel he was beginning to regard them as personal enemies.

Why? Mark looked at his gloved hands. There was no chance that he or Godspel could become infected, and Lawrence had telephoned again to say that the Scottish outbreak appeared to be over. No further victims had been reported. The dead were buried in quicklime and in a few days the area would be re-opened and declared safe. The danger was past, his inquiries were academic, and he should try to relax.

Relax! What a damn-fool command, Mark thought. Though one outbreak had waned, there might be others in the offing and the origin was all-important; also the destination. Why had the disease suddenly appeared in a remote corner of the British Isles? If a mad scientist of fiction were responsible he would have released his monsters on a crowded city.

*Why – if – where from – how –* and *how many?* How many estab-
lishments similar to Rushton Park were dotted around the world?
At least four in the United States and probably more in the Soviet
Union. One in France, two in West Germany and many others he
didn't know about – many, many others. If the strain was artificial,
it had almost certainly come from some government-sponsored
research station, so how had it escaped? How had it travelled so
far? How had the spores remained dormant till they reached the
Ben Sagur peninsula and struck?

But if he could find that out, he might have an inkling of the
time factors. Mark had told the switchboard to put the expected
call through on the intercom and the buzzer was sounding. He
pressed the answering button and listened to a voice. The voice of
a man who was young, but as self-opinionated and self-assured as
Admiral Archibald Fetherstone.

'You are certain?' The statement had been so definite that
Mark raised his eyebrows. 'The date can be pinpointed to the very
month?'

'I have just said so, Sir Marcus.' The informant obviously
resented his doubts. 'The calculation of age by solving the equa-
tion $(½)t/T = B/A$ is an exact science, and Professor Abraham
Hailey-Cohen's recently developed oscilloscope screens have made
it a rapid one. I'll give a couple of examples.

'If you believed a fragment of timber belonged to the True
Cross, we could support or dispel that belief by stating whether
the carbon elements were contemporary with Jesus Christ. The
same applies to much older substances.' He paused to think of
a more dramatic revelation. 'Say a fossilized bone of *Stegosaurus
unglatus*; the cretaceous armoured dinosaur. I'd substantiate its age
to within the odd thousand years.

'With modern data the problem is even simpler, the time factors narrower, and you can accept my findings without hesitation.
The spores I have examined originally germinated during the last
two weeks of September, 1970.'

'Thank you, Mr . . .' Mark's memory had returned and his
excitement was on the boil. 'Sorry – I don't know your name, but
I'm extremely grateful.'

'My name is Dr . . .' The man started to state his identity with some pride, but Mark had already switched off the set and he didn't hear him. He hardly heard Edgar Godspel drop the whisky glass, stammer out an excuse and hurry to the door. All he heard clearly was the voice in his head and the statement that voice had made. All he could concentrate on was that voice, that statement and a date.

A key date – September, 1970. The month in which Emily Repton had been appointed to her present job; and one of her remarks was a key one.

'Experiments at Rushton Park produced similar results . . .'

## Fourteen

There couldn't – couldn't be a connection. The dates were pure chance. Edgar Godspel tried to reassure himself in the taxi which he'd been lucky to find. It was midnight, rain was falling heavily and the gutters were flowing like miniature streams.

A coincidence – just another coincidence, and what a fool he was. A panic-stricken imbecile who had rushed out of the laboratory muttering that a wartime injury was troubling him and he had to go home. A credible reason, because he had been blown up during the blitz and suffered abdominal damage. Part of his stomach and a length of intestine had been removed and he often experienced pain after heavy meals or too much alcohol. Mark Levin knew that and he would accept the excuse, though it wasn't true. Edgar Godspel had no physical discomfort – he was mentally on edge.

On edge? What an understatement! He was terrified and sickened, because the time factors were too exact for coincidence. There had to be a link and his conviction strengthened as the miles slid by.

'What was that, sir?' He had spoken aloud and the driver inclined an ear to the partition panel. 'I'm afraid I didn't catch what you said.'

'Nothing – nothing important.' Godspel struggled to sound normal. 'I was just remarking on the weather.'

'Beastly isn't it.' The man nodded in agreement. 'Though I suppose the farmers will be pleased. A long, dry spell and then torrents of rain. The roads are like ruddy skating-rinks and that's why I'm going a bit slowish. Hope you're not in a hurry, sir.'

'No, I'm not in any hurry.' That was a partly accurate statement, Godspel thought. He had to know whether he was right or wrong, but he had no wish to hear the truth – he dreaded confirmation. He dreaded the meeting which was about to take place. In his heart of hearts he knew that his suspicions were correct. They were also unspeakable. *A hollow man – a stuffed man.* Eliot's poem described his character and career. He was empty and relied on pretences to hide the vacuum; jokes and feigned cheerfulness and the assurance of alcohol. A pocket Nero fiddling tunelessly away, though he had never guessed that Rome was still burning. Until tonight he'd been quite sure that the embers were dead and blackened and harmless.

'Could you direct me, sir?' The driver spoke through the panel again. 'I think we're getting close, but I don't know this district well.'

'Take the third turning on the right. You can't miss it, because there's a big pub at the corner.' If only that pub were open, Godspel thought. If only I'd asked the porter to buy a full bottle of Scotch instead of a half. If only I'd got the remains of that half bottle with me.

There would be plenty to drink when he reached his destination, but not whisky. A bitter draught – wine from the cup of Gethsemane.

And here was Gethsemane. The taxi had stopped beside a lamp post and he climbed out, thrust a ten-pound note into the driver's hand and walked off through the rain without waiting for his change.

Money was of no importance to him any more – only fear was important. Fear he had created himself.

A monster from his own brain was on the rampage.

\*   \*   \*

'The last one please, Jean.' Mark felt his usual repugnance as he nodded at the caged monkeys. Though they were necessary he always hated experiments on animals. For all he knew, they had as much right to life and divine mercy as himself; maybe more right. He had hurt a great many people in his time. Some deliberately, some accidentally and at least one – a much loved one, by stupidity and lack of foresight. He had taken his first wife, Rachel, on an expedition to the Far East, and she had died in a jungle because his medical kit contained no antibiotic to check the commonplace bug that killed her.

Who had the monkeys hurt? Why did the wretched beasts deserve pain, deformity and premature death? Because they lacked immortal souls?

Rubbish, Mark told himself, reaching for a hypodermic syringe and filling it from one of the culture saucers. The soul was an unproven substance; power was the answer. The survival of the fittest – the strong preying on the weak and using them for their own ends.

In this instance the end was the need for scientific information, and an unfortunate, frightened animal might provide him with an answer. Might tell him exactly what had caused the sickness on the Ben Sagur peninsula. Whether there could be a connection between that outbreak and something which had happened in a government research station five years ago.

'Steady, Jacko. Steady, boy.' Jean Hedges, the lab assistant who had replaced Godspel, was a big, muscular girl, but she was having to struggle to pull the little Rhesus monkey out on to the bench. 'He almost seems to know what may be in store for him, Sir Marcus.'

'They all seem to know, Jean.' This was the third animal to be treated and they'd each shown the same signs of convulsive terror. Trembling and gibbering and cowering back in the cages. Pathetic spectacles, but there was no time for sentiment. If another epidemic was remotely possible, Mankind, the Lord of the Ages, must have weapons to fight it. The monkey was under control now and Mark lifted the syringe, probed for a vein and pressed the plunger.

'No, I haven't a notion how long the incubation period is, Jean, or when we'll see any symptoms.' He shrugged at the girl's question and watched her release the infected animal. It scurried back into the cage and crouched shivering against the bars. 'All I know is that the strain started to develop – or to be developed – five years ago.'

Five years, almost to a week, if the isotope tests were as accurate as he'd been told. Mark suspected that the time factor was important, but he did not suspect that distance was equally vital. Approximately five miles from the hospital another hypodermic plunger had just forced a culture home. But not into a monkey's bloodstream.

The vein it entered was human.

# Fifteen

Five years ago something had happened at Rushton Park which Emily Repton considered might – just might – have a bearing on current events. Only a possibility, but the time factors tallied and the incidents had to be compared.

Mark's Ferrari glided silently along the motorway. Though normally a fast driver, he kept in the slow, inner lane; partly to concentrate and partly because he was exhausted. He had got home at four o'clock in the morning and almost literally dropped into bed beside Tania. But after two hours the telephone had woken them and he'd heard Kathleen Godspel's voice. She had rung St Bede's and been told that Edgar was seen leaving around midnight, but she'd had no word from him and was desperately worried.

Mark had tried to be helpful, though he was half-asleep and his eyes ached through peering into the microscopes. He'd only partially taken in Godspel's muttered excuse about stomach cramps and imagined he was going home. If the pain had become worse during the journey, he would probably have stopped at one of the two hospitals on the way: Charterfield's or Queen Elizabeth's. Mark had advised the woman to contact their casualty departments and also the police, because one had to be practical as well as kind.

Edgar Godspel had downed nearly half a bottle of Scotch in the laboratory. Not a large amount for a heavy drinker, but he might have had more before, and more afterwards. That was the probable reason for his absence. He'd started off home, his discomfort grew worse and a source of relief other than medicine had occurred to him. He'd gone to a nightclub, drunk himself insensible and ended up in a police cell. He'd been involved in an accident, or lost his memory.

Each explanation was possible, Mark thought, but he wasn't Edgar Godspel's nursemaid and he'd been too preoccupied to pay much attention to what Tania had told him about the man's past tragedy. An old flame named Annabel Lee who had vanished shortly before his present marriage. A girl whose picture was displayed on his mantelpiece. A girl whom Tania thought she had known, though Kathleen Godspel assured her it was unlikely.

No, Mark hadn't paid much attention to Tania, and Godspel's problems, physical or psychological, were no concern of his. Edgar Godspel had let him down and he'd had to enlist a junior lab assistant to help him finish the work – work he loathed. He hated condemning animals to torture, and the torture should be apparent by the time he returned to St Bede's. When he opened that locked room, he would hear the creatures whimpering.

A very securely locked room and its key was in Mark's pocket. The culture saucers would still be swarming and even to finger their rims without protective gloves might be suicide.

Gloves – gloves that had to be washed in disinfectant before they were removed and touched by the naked hand. Gloves which he and Godspel and Jean Hedges had worn. Though Mark was driving slowly a sudden anxiety struck him and he almost missed the turn-off to Rushton. Edgar Godspel had hurried out of the laboratory complaining of stomach cramps. Was it possible that sudden pain had made him forget the risks and pulled off his gloves without disinfecting them? If so, his disappearance might not be due to stomach trouble or alcohol.

Quite out of the question. Edgar Godspel was a scientist and he knew what was involved. However intense his spasms he would never have forgotten to take that precaution. Nor could any disease show its results so quickly. Mark dismissed the possibility as the signs loomed up before him. RUSHTON PARK RESEARCH ESTAB-LISHMENT – NO ADMISSION TO UNAUTHORIZED PERSONS – GUARD DOG PATROL. Godspel had not picked up the virus – others had. The poor, inoffensive little beasts he'd deliberately infected.

Poor, inoffensive, little beasts! Far, far behind him those beasts were at work. Paws and claws and teeth tugging at the bars, bodies thrusting against the cage doors. But they did not squeak or whimper in agony as Mark imagined. They snarled and grunted and growled and they were not like any Rhesus monkeys. Much much bigger animals were struggling to escape, and freedom was only one of their motives.

They wanted to get at each other.

'What was a Cornish postman doing here; two hundred and thirty miles from his home and his depot?' A police inspector was talking to a police surgeon. 'Where was he heading for and why did he kill himself? A stupid accident, or suicide? I think we can rule out murder.'

'Can we?' The doctor looked down at Harry Lloyd's body on the mortuary slab – what was left of it. Four gallons of petrol had produced formidable destruction and Lloyd had only been identified by his metal identification disc and the particulars of the van.

'I don't think we can rule out anything at this juncture, Inspector. No sane man would open a petrol tin and light a cigarette. Only masochists and religious fanatics kill themselves by fire. Buddhist monks have done so, but a level-headed English postman . . .' The doctor shrugged. A telephone call to Lloyd's supervisor had given them a sketch of the man's character. Hard-working, efficient, unimaginative and a valued employee who had served the Post Office for twenty-six years. A devoted husband and the father of three grown-up children who appeared to think highly of him. A popular colleague and the captain of the local darts team. Not at all the kind of person to make a stupid mistake or go out of his mind.

'It might have been murder.' The doctor puffed at his pipe to stifle the reek of putrid flesh, and tried to form a theory. Could Lloyd have been forced to drive to the Midlands? By a criminal with a gun perhaps who made off when the tank ran dry? Fair enough but that didn't explain the explosion, and it was highly irregular for a postman to carry inflammable substances in his van.

'Yes, it might have been murder,' he repeated. 'Someone could have substituted petrol for a harmless liquid; paraffin or water . . .'

'Or piss, Doc, because that's what you're talking.' The inspector prided himself on calling a spade a spade and being a rough diamond. *Rough* was correct, but no precious stone gleamed beneath his rugged exterior. 'If Lloyd believed the tin contained water or paraffin, why was he preparing to pour the stuff into an empty petrol tank? Why should he bother to lift the tin out of the van in the first place? What was he hoping to do with it?'

'Those are questions we may never know, Inspector, and I apologize for talking, or, as you put it, spouting urine.' The doctor was used to his colleague's manners and had taken no offence. 'But my job is to determine the cause of death and I want much more information before I issue a certificate.'

'Surely the cause is obvious!' The policeman was also staring down at the slab and he could hardly imagine what Harry Lloyd had looked like when he was alive. The corpse had been swollen by the heat and it had no hair, no eyebrows and very little skin. 'The man went off his rocker and committed suicide. He was killed by an explosion and multiple burns. We can see the evidence here and now, and we've heard what the lorry crew had to say.'

'There's no doubt what finally killed him, Inspector, and you may be right about his mental state.' The doctor nodded. 'A brainstorm leading to panic and suicide. But I still intend to perform a detailed autopsy.' He stooped till his eyes were almost touching the corpse. In spite of the mutilations there was something familiar about its facial features. Something he had seen in a textbook a long time ago – probably during his student days. Something disturbing, though it had nothing to do with sudden death. The symptoms were prolonged.

'I think it's possible that this man was dying before he lit the petrol.'

'We're doing well, Pete, and the series is coming along better than anyone could have expected.' Denis Rodgers, features editor of the *Western Weekly Advertiser and Clarion*, grinned at Peter Clarke, his photographer and close friend. 'Damn well, and let's hope this buzzard is the nuttiest of the lot.'

'Then he'll have to be a raving lunatic.' Clarke smiled gleefully back at him, because they had reason to be pleased with themselves. The series in question was to be entitled 'Our Notable Local Eccentrics' and some very queer customers had been interviewed already.

A retired major of the Royal Engineers, who'd invented a perpetual motion machine . . . A Church of England canon who assured them that the Ancient Britons were the lost tribe of Israel and Christ had visited Cornwall while serving as ship's carpenter on a Phoenician galley . . . A clairvoyant undertaker with a helpful spirit guide who foretold death and kept him prepared for business . . . A cattle farmer who considered sheep the familiars of Satan and warned them against eating mutton or wearing wool next to the skin . . . A district nurse – the reincarnation of Florence Nightingale, Edith Cavel or Marie Stopes. She wasn't sure which. Possibly all, but definitely one of those ladies.

Yes, the series should be most entertaining and all the subjects had been willing to be photographed and have their claims expressed in print. Willing and eager, though the major had declined to show his apparatus at work.

'Too secret – too important and hush-hush, gentlemen,' he had said laying a finger on his lips and beaming proudly at a complicated arrangement of cogs and pulleys and flywheels. 'After a few simple adjustments that machine is going to restore Britain's economy and we mustn't let the ruddy Chinks and Russkis in on it.'

All very satisfactory; first-rate copy. Only one more eccentric was needed to complete the articles and the mysterious Dr Carlin should fit the bill. A hermit – a recluse – who had appeared out of the blue five years ago, was rude to visitors and walked the moors muttering loudly to himself. There must be an odd bee in his bonnet, a bat in his belfry, to regale the *Advertiser's* readers, if he could be persuaded to talk.

'Here we are, Pete, so let's hope the bleeder's at home and ready to co-operate.' Rodgers stopped the car beside the stile that Harry Lloyd had climbed and the two journalists stepped cheerfully out – one with his shorthand pad, one with his camera. They were delighted with their efforts, but though they didn't know it, Dr Allan Carlin would not appear in 'Our Notable Local Eccentrics'. He was far too important for the little *Advertiser*.

Before long, almost every major newspaper in the world would publish the story they were about to tell.

## Sixteen

'A bad business, Sir Marcus, though as I told Colonel Lawrence at the time, there are no written records available.' Emily Repton's office at Rushton Park was modern in the extreme, but Mr David Locke, the senior administration officer, clashed with the surroundings. A tall, white-haired man with a wing collar, a black coat and grey striped trousers. He made Mark think of an illustration of a country solicitor for a book by Mrs Gaskell.

'The security guard was asleep when the outrage occurred and we found that he had been drinking before going on duty. I naturally gave him his cards the next morning. Triggs, I think the fellow's name was. Yes, Donald Triggs – a most unsatisfactory individual.'

'We are interested in the actual experiments, Mr Locke.' Emily Repton was perched on the edge of a stainless-steel chair, her hooped back looking even more deformed in a sitting position. 'The team were engaged in viral mutations, weren't they?'

'That is correct, Professor, but I'm not a scientist like yourself and Sir Marcus.' Locke had a respect for learning and he bowed to his superior and pronounced Mark's title with a flourish. 'I took in few of the details and was told very little. Dr Carlin, the head of the group, was a reticent old gentleman. Some people thought him ill-mannered, but I found him pleasant enough till the end. Understandable that he should have been crotchety. Failure sours all of us.

'But as for Frederick Brown, Carlin's second-in-command.'
Locke's eyebrows were as white as his hair and they came up in a
bar across his domed forehead. 'A brilliant man, I suppose, but they
always say that the best minds are the first to crack, Sir Marcus.

'What an unfortunate remark.' Locke flushed at his lack of
tact. 'Probably a false one too, though there's no doubt in my own
mind that Brown was unbalanced. An arrogant, self-opinionated
young puppy who was largely responsible for everything that went
wrong. He made himself scarce as soon as the inquiry was over
and my guess is that he's come to a sticky end.'

'Your guess is correct, Mr Locke.' Mark knew that the pieces
of the puzzle were fitting together, and not only the time factors
tallied. A technician called Frederick Brown had been the first carrier of the Ben Sagur epidemic. 'Brown probably died in extreme
agony.'

'I'm sorry to hear that.' Locke flushed again, but only for a second. 'No, I'm not sorry – I'm glad. I disliked Fred Brown intensely
and *de mortuis nil nisi bonum*, is an absurd command. Should one
speak well of Hitler and Stalin merely because they happen to be
dead? Must one praise Caligula and Nero and the Borgias?'

'I share your view, Mr Locke, but may we get down to the facts?'
Mark finished the cup of tea Emily Repton had offered him. Weak,
China tea which had done nothing to relieve his tiredness. 'What
was the end-product of the experiments? New vaccine strains?'

'Far more ambitious than that, sir.' Locke shook his head. 'Carlin described the project as a *lifeline*, and Brown once told me that
they would "save future generations from starvation". A pompous
man and a malicious liar to boot. It was Brown who suggested that
Miss Lee stole the data and fled to Russia.'

'Miss Lee?' Mark remembered what Tania had tried to tell him
and another piece of the puzzle had clicked into place. 'Annabel
Lee?'

'Of course, Sir Marcus. You've obviously read about the case,
though we all called her Annie.' Locke's lips creased into a nostalgic
smile. 'Such a lovely girl. So appealing and warm and intelligent. If
I had a daughter I hope she'd have been like dear little Annie.

'She had a very pleasant boyfriend too. Extremely pleasant,

though a bit older than herself. I can't remember his name, but she introduced me to him and I gathered that they were getting engaged.' The smile turned to a scowl. 'Fred Brown knew that too, but he was always pestering the girl . . . forcing his unwelcome attentions on her.' Mr Locke's speech was as archaic as his dress and Mark stifled a grin.

'A vicious brute, Sir Marcus. One day in the laboratory, Annie finally told him that she found him physically and mentally repellent and he slapped her face.' Locke had loose dentures and they clicked in indignation. 'Being a spirited lass, she obviously struck back at him and I gather there was quite a scuffle till Dr Carlin came on the scene. The doctor was naturally furious and told Brown that he'd get his marching orders if he ever bothered her again. I saw Brown in the canteen after the incident and if ever a man had murder in his face . . .'

'Mr Locke.' Professor Repton interposed again. 'Sir Marcus is not interested in the team's personalities, but their work. What was Dr Carlin's actual aim? How did he try to carry it out and what went wrong?'

'I don't really know, madam. As I said, I'm not a scientist, but in my view . . .'

*In my opinion – in my belief – in my view.* Locke claimed ignorance and humility, but they were false claims. While he listened, Mark's weariness faded and he realized why Emily Repton had mentioned the incident to him at Liskerg.

Two men and a woman working on a project to solve the world's food crisis. A project that had been abandoned hurriedly, though the idea was a good one.

Mutated filter viruses aggravating and strengthening the glandular system. The overactive glands producing changes in the rest of the body: immunity to disease, intensely rapid growth and giantism; super animals. Rabbits larger than pigs – pigs as big as cattle.

A laudable attempt, but it failed, and Locke didn't know why. The experimental subjects, rats and guinea-pigs, had been given lethal injections and incinerated. Carlin and Brown tendered their resignations. Annabel Lee went on the sick-list and vanished.

On the day after her disappearance someone broke into the laboratory, destroyed the equipment and removed the written records.

Who had broken in? Mark wondered. Frederick Brown seemed the chief suspect. A violent, unstable man who had later sought employment with James Fraser Clyde. Brown would have had ample research facilities in Clyde's laboratories. If Brown had the records he might have decided to resume the experiments, and have suffered accordingly.

'Not Brown, Sir Marcus.' Mr Locke answered his question reluctantly. 'The man had a cast-iron alibi, as the police put it. He was at a cocktail party at the time of the break-in. And not Annie either. The poor child was ill and running a high temperature. She had influenza and had been ordered to bed.'

'Yet she left her bed and vanished.' Mark's tiredness had also vanished. Another section of the jigsaw was fitting together and he imagined how it might have been. *Hoist with your own petard – caught in your own web – stewed in your own juice*, were the apt phrases. The experiments were abandoned because they created uncontrollable, contagious monsters, and Annabel Lee was one of them. Only a theory, but worth considering.

The poor child, as Locke rightly called her, had become infected by the strain she and her colleagues were working on and gone berserk. She had returned to the laboratory, smashed everything there was to smash and then hurried away to die.

A cave, a hole in the ground, a deserted building, a stretch of woodland. Anywhere where she could be alone with her agony, and she had died and lain there unnoticed. Quite harmless, till one unlucky day, someone discovered the long-dead corpse, and touched its withered flesh. The house of the enemy – Pandora's box containing the spores that did not die.

'Good grief.' The telephone had rung, Emily Repton was listening to the caller and the urgency of her tone interrupted Mark's thoughts. 'Yes, he's with me now. I'll hand you over to him.' She motioned to Mark. 'Colonel Lawrence.'

'Have you found a cure for that bug yet, old boy?' Bill Lawrence sounded even tenser than he had been at St Bede's or Clanross

Grange or Liskerg and Mark's negative answer produced a string of repetitive obscenities.

'Then you and the bloody Repton woman and all the other bloody boffins had better get off your bloody arses and do some bloody work. We were sure that the Scottish outbreak had been contained and obliterated, but it seems we're wrong.' The colonel was not only tense – he was strident.

'A body with the same symptoms has been found in the Midlands.'

'Yes, I think so.' Samuel Kahn, the Chairman of Global Newspapers, laid down one of the Instamatic photographs Peter Clarke had taken at Merrytor Cottage. 'In fact I'm virtually sure.'

Clarke and Rodgers were hard-headed young men and in spite of their initial shock they had kept their wits about them. After taking the pictures they had telephoned the police from a call-box and then hurried to the *Weekly Advertiser's* office to talk to their editor.

The editor, another hard-headed character, had at once realized that he was on to a good thing and the pictures and Rodgers' notes had been rushed to London by motorcycle.

'The symptoms are the same that Clyde showed us on the projector screen, but much clearer.' Kahn prided himself on being unflappable, but he was in a flap now. 'The only illustration of a living subject was a poor exposure and the corpses had been burned.'

'This man – if it was a man – looks hardly human, sir.' John Forest was holding a magnifying glass over a close-up print. Even in death and with a sword protruding through its chest the thing appeared menacing. The face contorted, and the half-naked body so bloated that he couldn't determine whether it had been male or female. 'But *virtually* sure is not good enough, sir. Are you certain?'

'Yes, I'm certain as I know I'm a Yid, John.' The pictures had shaken Kahn badly. He had been about to leave for the theatre when Forest telephoned him and, though he'd removed his dinner-jacket, his dress-shirt was damp with sweat. 'That's another example of the Scottish illness, so what do we do?'

'What do *you* do, sir.' Forest had seen enough and he lowered the glass. 'We have received official sanction to publish a brief account of Clyde's suicide and the Ben Sagur business tomorrow, but guardedly and with assurances that the danger is over and there is no cause for concern.'

'Over? When the epidemic has travelled more than five hundred miles!' Kahn had calculated the approximate distance from Liskerg to Cornwall. 'When it is probably spreading while we're talking here?

'No cause for alarm, indeed! Not to worry, because the outbreak was contained in time! The authorities were wrong on every count and we've got to come to a decision.'

Sam Kahn had been in the newspaper business all his adult life and he knew the penalties for issuing restricted information. A crippling fine on the *Globe* and the possibility of a prison sentence for himself and Forest. He also knew the danger of panic, and he was a public-spirited man. He had a hard choice to make. 'People have a right to know the truth, John; to be warned in advance.'

'I entirely agree, sir, and I think we should run the story for the public good.' Forest nodded at two sheets of headed notepaper on the desk. 'But that is only my personal view. The opinion of an employee, and the decision must be yours.'

Unlike Kahn, fat John Forest was not public-spirited and he had no interest in the public good. He took care of Number One, the only good that interested him was his own, and he had no intention of risking imprisonment. If anyone carried the can, it would be Sam Kahn.

'I need written orders, sir, so would you sign one of those notes now, because there isn't much time.' He glanced at his watch. 'We have a deadline to keep.'

'Publish or suppress.' Kahn consulted his own watch. He had read both letters carefully; the early editions of the paper would soon be going to bed, but he still hesitated. Not because of the penalties involved, though they were severe enough. Not for fear of missing a worldwide scoop. He wanted to take the right action, but he didn't know what was right. Deliver facts and risk panic and unrest – or keep silent?

Logic could not help him, and instinct guided Kahn's hand. He reached for his jacket, took a fountain pen from the inside pocket and bent over the desk.

'Very well, John,' he said, signing his name with a flourish. 'Those are my orders, so get on with them.'

## Seventeen

'Only coffee please, Tania, and make it black.' Barbiturates had given Mark a sound night's sleep, but he had no appetite. The situation was so serious that the idea of breakfast nauseated him.

After leaving Rushton Park he had driven to a town in the Midlands and confirmed Bill Lawrence's statement. The postman's body displayed the same symptoms of deformity, and the disease had not been contained. It had broken through the cordon and headed south.

There was still no news of Edgar Godspel either, which was disturbing. Though Mark thought it unlikely that Godspel could have been infected during their session in the St Bede's laboratory, the possibility had to be considered and the authorities were anxious about him. Godspel had not gone home, and he had not been admitted to any police station or casualty department. He appeared to have vanished into thin air.

Just as a girl Godspel knew in the past had vanished. Annabel Lee, who'd complained of flu or a heavy cold, left her sickbed and was never seen again. There'd been rumours that she might have defected to the Soviet bloc, but Lawrence, who was in charge of the investigation, soon rejected them. Her passport was in a dressing-table drawer and no Western agent had reported her presence behind the Iron Curtain. Pretty Annie Lee was probably dead. She had vanished without a trace and her colleagues had left Rushton as soon as the inquiry was finished.

Though Frederick Brown had not died – at least, not then. He had turned up like the proverbial bad penny; one of James Clyde's technicians and the first victim of the disease. The first carrier – maybe the originator.

*Into thin air – without a trace – a bad penny.* Like Clyde, Mark despised himself for thinking in clichés, but he had learned English from a teacher who revelled in them.

*A bad penny!* Also, *a fly in the ointment, the worm in the wheat, the nigger in the woodpile.* Three more terms with the same meaning, and three people had been involved in those Rushton Park experiments. Frederick Brown was definitely dead now, Annabel Lee had probably died five years ago, but what about the third? Dr Allan Carlin, the leader of the research team? Mr Locke believed Carlin had moved to Cornwall, Mark had advised Lawrence to trace him but was it possible that . . . ?

Mark finished his coffee and got up from the table. The copy of *Life and History* was still in the sitting-room and he opened the magazine at a group photograph and a line of names. There was Clyde, there was Weber, there was Frederick Brown, *and several* others. The reporter had compiled a comprehensive list of the Smilin' Boy's imported henchmen, but no Carlin was included. Probably the man was also dead, or living innocently in retirement. If he was alive he would have to be questioned, but that was Lawrence's business, not his. He had humbler witnesses to interview.

And they should be ready to give their evidence. The infected animals at St Bede's were bound to be showing signs of the sickness by now and it was time to examine them.

'No more coffee, thank you, darling. I must get along.' Mark came back into the dining-room. 'Why don't you pay Kathleen Godspel a call later in the day? The poor woman is obviously worried out of her mind and can do with a spot of company.

'Company, but not confidences, though.' Mark had seen panic-stricken mobs and he knew what rumour and gossip could do. 'Everything I've told you must remain secret, but you might be able to get some useful information from Mrs Godspel.' He paused because a sudden thought had struck him. 'Ask her to tell you all she can about Edgar's relationship with Annabel Lee. It could be important.

'Goodbye for the present, Tania. I don't know when I'll be back, but I promise you that there's no need to worry.' Mark crossed to the hall and took his coat and umbrella from a rack. The sky was darkening and St Bede's car-park was some distance from the entrance. He didn't want to risk a drenching and a dose of flu.

Flu; the key word, but he would beat it. He had to, because if he failed, humanity was in for an epidemic as serious as any of the great plague visitations of the past. A cure and an antidote would be found and time was the only problem. The creature must be tamed quickly.

Mark felt supremely confident of victory as he put on his coat, picked up the umbrella and kissed Tania. A confidence that turned to shock when he reached the front door and noticed the newspapers lying on the mat. The *Daily Globe's* heading made him stop dead and the umbrella almost dropped from his hand. He hardly heard the telephone ring or saw Tania go to answer it.

'The fools,' he said. 'The stupid, irresponsible, criminal fools.'

Mark Levin was not the only one to register shock. At about the same time as himself, several million other people were looking at the *Globe* and their reactions were all pretty much the same. Disbelief, followed by anger, disgust, fear and horror.

John Forest was a skilled sensationalist and he and his assistants had altered the journal's normal format to emphasize the crisis. Apart from a map, two photographs and a four-inch headline the front page was blank.

The pictures were the most gruesome of the collection taken in Carlin's cottage and the map showed the northwest coast of Scotland. The headline was printed in scarlet and consisted of a single word. PESTILENCE.

'Yes, I have seen the *Daily Globe* and glanced through Mr Forest's irresponsible article, but I have no comment to make.' Mark's arrival at St Bede's had been awaited and a group of reporters jostled around him as he mounted the steps to the portico. 'I repeat, no comment whatsoever, so will you please get out of my way?

'Oh, you're one of the jackals from the *Globe*, are you.' He brandished his umbrella at a persistent individual on the top step.

'Then, if you don't let me pass you'll get this across your face.'
Mark was not normally given to violence, but Forest's leakage still
infuriated him, and the threat might well have been fulfilled if two
commissionaires had not hurried out to intervene.

'Stand aside, gentlemen. Sir Marcus has work to do.' Burly,
uniformed authority succeeded where he had failed. The group
parted, and Mark walked quickly through the doorway and across
the entrance hall.

The commissionaire was right, he thought in the privacy of the
lift. The telephone call Tania had taken was from a Ministry of
Health official who confirmed the Globe's story. The body found
in the Cornish cottage displayed the same tell-tale symptoms and
a lot of hands had touched it. The police, the ambulance crew and
the staff of a mortuary. They were all being kept in strict isolation,
but what could be done to protect them?

At the moment the answer was nothing, and Mark considered
James Clyde. A fanatic and a megalomaniac, but at least he had
realized the nature of the scourge and shown some commonsense.
The Scottish corpses had been externally sterilized by flames and
the same applied to the dead postman.

But the Cornish body had not been subjected to heat. A sword-
thrust had killed its owner and the skin was probably seething
with the contaminating spores. A serum had to be found quickly,
and three little Rhesus monkeys were the only informants he had.

Only three informants, but a host of interrogators, and after
Mark left the lift and set off down the long corridor the questions
were shot at him. One and a half million people bought the *Daily
Globe* regularly and four times that number read it. That was on a
normal day and today was far from normal. Everyone had seen or
been told about those pictures on the front page and the lurid article that filled the middle section. Everyone knew he was involved
and they were eager for news. Housemen and consultants, stu-
dents and nurses and radiologists. Everyone he passed tried to
question him, and even Dr Paulton-Oakes, the Dean of the Hospital tried to halt his progress with a lordly, beckoning arm. Mark
ignored them all and hurried to the ante-room of the laboratory.

But he didn't go into the lab straight away. Two pairs of hands were needed and he turned on the intercom and asked the receptionist to have Jean Hedges sent up.

'Miss Hedges hasn't reported for duty yet, Sir Marcus. A lot of the staff are late this morning. The younger members mostly, and it's quite unpardonable.' Mark knew the woman well. A dour old battleaxe without a good word for anybody, but he warmed towards her as he had warmed to Emily Repton at Liskerg. She was obviously quite unflappable and the *Globe's* scare edition had not perturbed her.

'However, Jean Hedges is a fairly reliable girl and I'm sure she'll be along soon. I'll send her up to you immediately and . . .' There was a brief pause. 'I'd also like to wish you the best of luck, sir.'

'Thank you, Mrs Howell. Thank you very much. Luck is a commodity we can all use.' Mark switched off the set, and looked at his watch before crossing to the lab door. Jean Hedges was a punctual and reliable girl, and she was late – half an hour late. Was there the slightest chance that her delay and Godspel's disappearance had the same cause?

Out of the question. Edgar Godspel knew the danger. He would never have removed his gloves without taking the proper precautions, and Mark had seen Jean disinfect hers. Godspel was probably suffering from loss of memory and there must be an innocent reason for the girl's delay. Oversleeping – a delay on a bus or a train – an indisposition. She'd be on duty in a few minutes. If not, he'd have to send for another assistant.

An indisposition! Perhaps a cold or a touch of flu? Shivers and aches and a slight temperature. Those were the symptoms Annabel Lee had complained of before she vanished, and the germ was almost certainly a mutated influenza virus. If Jean phoned to say she was experiencing anything of the kind, the coincidence could not be ignored. She might also be too ill to telephone and he'd better call her flat. Mark turned to the intercom again, but the buzzer whirred before he pressed the switch, and he heard Mrs Howell's voice.

'Miss Hedges has just arrived, sir, and is on her way to you. Apparently there is a go-slow on the District line.'

'Thank you, Mrs Howell.' Mark remembered the reporters who

had been clustered around the entrance. 'And I don't want to be disturbed this morning, so only put through calls which you consider to be urgent. I'm sure you can distinguish the sheep from the goats.'

He switched off the set and took a key from his pocket. Jean was all right, but he had to examine other individuals who would definitely be ill. He opened the laboratory door and took one step forward . . . only one.

In the autumn of 1970, someone had entered a laboratory at Rushton Park and destroyed its equipment and records. Five years later, a similar act of vandalism had been performed in London and Mark gasped at what he saw.

Culture saucers and test tubes lay shattered on the bench. Two of the microscopes had been hurled across the room, and the Bunsen burner dangled from its gas pipe. A filing cabinet had been overturned and the animal cages were empty. The bars had been wrenched apart to release their captives.

Who could have done it? The door was securely locked when he and Jean left and only he had a key. Who had removed the caged monkeys and killed them? He looked at the two bodies on the floor. They were both dead and appeared larger than they had done in life. They were also saturated with blood as though a maniac had taken a knife and repeatedly stabbed them.

A maniac or . . . Mark remembered that there was another key. The duty porters kept one for emergencies and any senior staff member could ask for it; a person like Edgar Godspel.

If Edgar had returned – if Edgar was responsible, the battle was approaching its climax. The people of Scotland had wantonly destroyed property and attacked each other like wild beasts. He had been wrong again. Edgar Godspel was infected and the outbreak was loose in London.

A frightening prospect and a personal threat, unless his eyes and ears were deceiving him. Unless the noise and the shadow were imaginary. Though the sky was dark outside the window and the room dim, Mark didn't turn on the lights. He stood quite still, and he realized that there was no deception. He was not alone and the noise was coming from behind a desk which had been pulled away from the wall. Not a loud sound, but full of menace and he thought he knew its source. Edgar Godspel was very close to him.

Mark never noticed Jean Hedges enter the ante-room and hang up her coat. He just listened and watched, reversed his grip on the umbrella to use the handle as a weapon. A poor weapon, but he had no time to look for another. The sound was growing louder, the shadow was hardening into a solid object, the enemy was emerging from its hiding-place.

A grunting, slobbering enemy he had helped to create.

## Eighteen

PESTILENCE! The word echoed in homes and offices and factories. In pubs and restaurants and trains and buses and aeroplanes. In shops and hotels and wherever men and women were gathered together. It also rang through the minds of solitary individuals.

PESTILENCE! A scourge sweeping across the British Isles and the death-toll already exceeded two hundred. Samuel Kahn had intended to plant a warning, but the harvest was far heavier and more bitter. Kahn was not merely regretting his decision to give Forest *carte blanche*. He would have forfeited half his declining years to push the clock back to the moment he'd signed that fatal letter.

Only two major facts had been left unpublished. Forest did not know about Godspel's disappearance or the way Harry Lloyd had died, but they were not necessary to boost his scoop. The photographs would have sufficed on their own, and the article suggested that the germ was a biological weapon and virtually unstoppable. Chaos had come and people were frightened.

'My sore throat!' 'Elsie's cough!' 'Dad's hay fever!'

'This shaking – that vomiting after breakfast! Maybe a hangover – did have a skinful last night, but . . .'

'Those headaches! The doctor said they were due to migraine, but if he was wrong . . .'

'I've got it – I know I've got it – and I can't stand pain. I'd rather go out quickly. Pills – sleeping-pills – how many are there left? Twenty – twenty should be enough.'

John Forest had a lot to answer for. Every doctor in the country had a queue outside his surgery, and the day's suicide rate was the highest on record.

People were angry and rebellious as well as frightened. If James Clyde was responsible, the authorities had been negligent. If they themselves had manufactured the weapon, they were criminals.

Within minutes of the *Globe's* appearance, telephone callers were arranging demonstrations outside Parliament and Downing Street and a mass march on Rushton Park was in the offing. By noon the Stock Market would have closed, the country's turn-out of workers quartered, and schools and colleges empty.

Why invest money, or slave away at a desk or a lathe or on a building site, if you're going to die? Why waste time in a class-room, if you're going to end up looking like something out of a horror movie? Better have a bit of fun or register your protest. Lay your wife or your girl-friend – go on the booze – march through the streets and beat up policemen. Why not smash a few windows and have a fight with those kids across the park? Fight, just for the fun of fighting.

A lot of fights took place during the day, but only two really mattered. One was Mark Levin's fight in the laboratory.

'Are you sure, sir?' Jean Hedges' face was pale with shock and her hands trembled as she put on a protective gown and a pair of gloves. 'Are you quite certain that you weren't scratched or bitten?'

'I am perfectly all right, Jean. It didn't get near me, so please try to control your nerves.'

An easy order to give, but a hard one to take, and Mark had to stifle nausea as he looked at the thing that had gone berserk in the laboratory. No human being had entered the room. An animal was responsible for the wreckage; an animal which had broken out of its cage, fought and killed both its companions when they followed suit, and smashed equipment in blind fury.

A monstrous, deformed animal; far, far bigger and more power-ful than any Rhesus monkey. The virus injections had acted much more rapidly and effectively than Mark had imagined possible. Glandular activity had enlarged the cell-tissue and strengthened the muscle-fibres, and it had bounded across the floor with the agility of a cornered rat. Mark would never forget the sight of those outstretched claws and bared teeth flying towards him before a lucky blow from the umbrella handle slammed home across its forehead.

'The brute's alive, thank God. I merely stunned him, but he'd better stay unconscious for a while.' Though the limbs were relaxed and the eyes closed, Mark could see that the creature was still breathing. 'Morphine, please, Jean. One and a half grains should keep him quiet.'

'You say, thank God, Sir Marcus?' The girl was still in a state of shock and thought she had misheard him. 'Give it a lethal dose and incinerate the carcass.'

'Burn the best evidence we've got?' Mark had also put on protective clothing and he stooped and lifted the hideous body on to a table. If those teeth or nails had found their targets he might have welcomed a quick death himself, but nausea was being replaced by curiosity and excitement.

'Just pull yourself together, Jean, and do what I say. We've got a living subject to study at last and I want to see what's going on inside him.

'I also want some outside information, so telephone Rushton Park and ask for the admin officer. A man called David Locke.' Mark had taken two empty syringes from a drawer, but he paused before extracting the blood samples he needed.

An idea had just struck him. Just a notion – a long shot. Probably the rankest outsider in the race, but worth checking. The parasite resisted any preparation which was not lethal to the host, but could something which wasn't a preparation in the accepted meaning of the term do the trick – something quite simple?

A faint possibility, and he considered his earlier examinations. Living spores had only been located in the inner organs of the victims. Heat had killed the exterior units, but could any of them have survived in certain unfavourable conditions? If not, his rank outsider might be first at the winning-post.

All the lines to Rushton are engaged, sir.' Jean Hedges replaced the receiver. 'Mrs Howell will keep trying and call you as soon as she gets through to Mr Locke.'

'Thanks.' Mark drew off a blood-sample from each of the dead animals and squirted them into test tubes. 'Now, would you nip along to the vaccine store and fetch these?' He wrote out a list of his requirements and handed it to her.

'Is that you, Mr Locke?' The telephone had rung as the girl closed the ante-room door behind her and Mark answered. 'I need some more details about the events we were discussing yesterday before Colonel Lawrence called and I left you.'

'I can't think about anything except present events, Sir Marcus.' Anxiety made Locke's false teeth click as loudly as indignation had done. 'Professor Repton and I are at our wits' ends. We've been trying to contact you ourselves, but the switchboard is jammed with incoming calls. Not only official calls, but from the Press and the public, and some of the latter have been abusive and threatening.

'I don't wonder that people are perturbed. I am myself, and now the police have told us to expect trouble during the afternoon. Demonstrations outside the complex, and possibly an actual attack on the place.

'What progress are you making, Sir Marcus? When will you be able to announce that an antidote is available? The professor's team has come up with nothing so far and the situation is desperate.'

'You don't have to tell me that, Mr Locke, and it will become far more desperate unless you can help me.' While he spoke, Mark was staring at the table, and what he saw horrified him. The drugged monkey's hair had started to shrivel. The fur was parting and falling away to reveal bald patches of skin.

'I have three questions to put to you, Mr Locke. Each reply is vital, so please cast your mind back to the time before Carlin's experiments . . . were abandoned. This is what I want to know.' He delivered the questions and waited for Locke's answers.

'Let me concentrate for a moment, Sir Marcus.' The man hesitated and Mark could picture him tapping his domed forehead. 'I think you're right and the girl was away for a couple of days. Fred Brown too, though I can't really be certain. I'll check the files and tell the switchboard to keep this line open so that I can call you back.

'As to your last enquiry . . .' There was another pause. 'Yes,

Carlin did give the project a code name; a longish and rather pretentious foreign title. I don't remember the exact words, but it was *La Dona* something or other.'

'Thank you, Mr Locke. Thank you very much indeed.' Mark lowered the phone and knelt down beside the third animal which lay near the door. His hunch – his rank outsider might be coming home.

'*La Señora Dona de España*; The Lady of Spain,' he said aloud. Though the corpse was male, its sex did not interest him. The unnatural grunting noise he had heard when he first entered the room had aroused his suspicions and Locke's reply could confirm them.

'The Lady . . . The Lady of Spain.' He repeated the phrase and then shouted out a warning as he heard the footsteps. A warning which was delivered too late.

Jean Hedges had returned carrying a rack of phials and she hadn't seen him. She stumbled slightly to avoid him and as she righted herself, her left shoe stepped on the umbrella Mark had dropped on the floor. Its handle twisted up and brushed against her stocking.

A wide-meshed stocking and the monkey had been wounded before killing its companions. There was a fair chance that the handle which had saved Mark's life was smeared with diseased blood.

## Nineteen

'I have never been one to underestimate the gravity of any situation, ladies and gentlemen, but I can assure you that there is no cause for alarm.' Mr Emrys Roberts, the Minister of Health, was usually a plausible liar, but he had lost his skill. While Tania watched his face on Kathleen Godspel's television screen, she knew that he was as alarmed as herself.

'It is correct that two hundred people have died. A heavy toll, but how many are killed on the roads every week of the year? It is also true that there was an outbreak of some unknown sickness, but how many hundred thousands die of conventional diseases every year?' He paused to let his audience consider the questions.

'And how many of the deaths which concern us were due to disease?' Before entering politics, the Minister had been a Welsh hill farmer and his voice wheedled, as though he was trying to knock down the price of a neighbour's sheep.

'A mere handful, my friends, and I have definite evidence that the majority of the victims were in normal health when they died.' Roberts took a sip from a glass at his side. The clear liquid it contained looked like water and some of it was. Water liberally laced with gin. 'So what are the true facts?

'I will tell you, ladies and gentlemen, and it is a very sad story.' He shook his head mournfully; an expression of disapproval which was usually reserved for his political opponents. 'Those unfortunate men and women were massacred. Sir James Fraser Clyde, an unbalanced would-be dictator with an army of hired thugs, went insane and ordered mass murder.

'Clyde later took his own life in a fit of remorse, but suicide will not pay for his crimes – not in a billion, billion years. The great judge of the universe counts every sparrow that falls, and a millstone shall be hanged about the sinner's neck.' Mr Roberts had also been a notable chapel preacher, but was inclined to mix and misquote biblical references.

'James Clyde must be held culpable for everything that has happened. He committed atrocities which we associate with the Nazis and he sealed off an area of British territory – your territory, my friends. But for Clyde, there would have been no epidemic whatsoever. The medical authorities would have found a cure for the illness long ago.

'And they will find one – rest assured of that. The germ responsible has already been isolated. Stocks of vaccine are being prepared and they will be issued if the situation requires such action.

'An unlikely action, so why have I interrupted the television programmes to talk to you? What is there to worry about?' He paused again and took another swig of gin and water – a much larger one.

'Your own minds are the worrying factors. Imagination inflamed by a single, sensation-seeking newspaper which thrives on distortion and deceit. Those are the only words to describe the

*Daily Globe*, and if its chairman, Samuel Kahn, wishes to sue me for slander he is welcome to try. The government will certainly be prosecuting him.' Mr Roberts leaned forward and smiled confidently at the camera, but the act did not work. Ninety-nine per cent of his viewers knew that he had no confidence at all.

'Those pictures, which many of you have seen this morning, are touched-up fakes. Obscene exaggerations to increase the *Daily Globe's* circulation. Attempts to swell the coffers of its shareholders by creating panic and unrest.

'Attempts which will fail, because we are not given to panic, as Adolf Hitler learned to his cost. The men and women of this country – the English, the Welsh, the Scots and . . . and our fellow citizens from overseas – do not panic.' He had been about to include the Irish, but opted for immigrants. During the night, I.R.A. bombs had wrecked a museum and an art gallery.

'No, the British people do not panic. We know each other too well even to consider that possibility, and there is no reason for panic.' He held out his hands in an expansive Celtic gesture which had won him several elections. 'A few unlucky individuals contracted a dangerous illness, but the cause of that illness will soon be known and rendered harmless. The best scientific brains will see to that, and I shall end with a piece of advice and a firm assurance.' Roberts closed his eyes for a moment and then opened them wide, as though personally studying the millions of faces looking at him.

'Relax and forget everything you saw in the *Globe*. Treat it with the contempt it deserves and go about your normal, everyday lives without fear or anxiety. You have my solemn promise that there is no cause for alarm. Nothing to worry about except your own imaginations.'

'What an unconvincing actor he is.' The screen had become blank, Kathleen Godspel was about to turn off the receiver, but she halted before pressing the switch. Another face had replaced Roberts's. A face she knew as well as her own.

'This is Dr Edgar Godspel who disappeared from St Bede's hospital in central London last Wednesday night. He is apparently suffering from loss of memory, and the police and the Ministry of Health wish to contact him.' The announcer's standard B.B.C. accent contrasted unfavourably with Roberts's attractive Welsh lilt. 'If anyone sees, or has seen Dr Godspel, do not approach him but contact Scotland Yard or your local police station.

'If you, yourself, are listening to me, Dr Godspel, please telephone St Bede's and ask for Sir Marcus Levin.'

'How can the poor devil telephone anybody?' The brief appeal was over and Kathleen switched off the set and shrugged her shoulders. 'Edgar's dead; dead and done with.

'Till this very moment I've been trying to reassure myself, Tania. To pretend that he was affected by drink or amnesia and he would come home.' She spoke in a whisper, but each word registered emotion. 'That I'd hear his key in the door and a ring on the phone.

'Every footstep in the street, every car that drew up sent me rushing to the window.' Though the woman wore heavier make-up than usual, Tania saw that her eyes were haunted and dark lines lay beneath the thick, pebble-glasses. 'I even kept searching the house in the hope that he might have crept in by the back door and I hadn't noticed him. I went from room to room, hoping and praying. How foolish I was.

'There's no hope. Edgar was drunk at the hospital. He neglected to take the necessary precautions and that finished him.'

'There's always hope, Kate.' Tania took her arm and led her back to a sofa. Though she was only twenty-nine and Kathleen Godspel must be at least fifty, the woman was so pathetic that she felt maternal as well as sympathetic towards her. A mother trying to console a troubled child. 'Mark is quite sure that Edgar could not have been infected in the laboratory.' The *Globe's* statements had made secrecy irrelevant, and before the television news she had told Kathleen all she knew.

'Then Mark is wrong, my dear.' Mrs Godspel lowered her stout, ungainly body on to the seat. 'Edgar was infected and he's dead.'

'We mustn't think that, Kate, though . . .' Tania checked herself because an image had crossed her mind. A man – half a man – hiding away in some empty building; diseased and deformed and lethal. An insane carrier who might soon be coming out to spread his sickness, if he hadn't done so already.

'You were about to say that it would be better if he had died.' Kathleen Godspel had read her thoughts. 'How right you are, Tania, though there's no need to worry on that score. Edgar was a humane person and an intelligent one.

'When he realized contagion had set in, he would have taken the only sensible course and killed himself. His corpse has probably floated out to sea already. Edgar knew the power of the Lady long before she reached Scotland. Edgar can't harm anyone any more.

'Nor is there any need for you to worry about me. I told you that I'm riddled with cancer and death will be a welcome friend.' The fingers of her left hand fondled Tania's right.

'Think of yourself, my dear. You and all the other beautiful, healthy people in the world. Consider them and pray that your Mark produces a serum in time. Forget me and forget Edgar. He's dead and I'm dying. We don't matter.'

'I don't want to forget, I have to remember, though I don't know why it's important.' Tania's eyes swung towards the photograph above the fireplace; Annabel Lee, a young attractive girl, whom she was sure she had met and talked to. Whom she had once been intimate with.

When – where – how? No, her memory did not respond, but there was a question that could be answered. 'Tell me, Kate,' she said. 'What did you mean by the *Lady*?'

Kathleen Godspel's statements had been more convincing than Mr Roberts's, but they were equally incorrect and there *was* cause for anxiety – great cause.

Dr Edgar Godspel had not died. He was very much alive: alive and kicking.

## Twenty

'You should be safe enough now, my dear.' Within seconds of Jean Hedge's contact with the umbrella Mark had made her wash her ankles in a solution of strong carbolic and then bandaged the area with lint soaked in more antiseptic. He had also examined the umbrella handle through a lens and found no traces of blood. 'I'm sorry I was so careless, but I think you can be regarded as a fair insurance risk.'

'As far as anyone can be.' The girl grimaced, because more disturbing news had just been received. Seven people were in isolation after handling the Cornish body and two of them, the ambulance driver and a nurse, were already showing signs of illness. 'But what were you saying before I tripped, sir? Something about a Spanish woman.'

'Not a woman, Jean. A lady and a very important one.' Jean Hedges was a qualified technician and Mark was surprised that she hadn't recognized the term at once. '*La Señora Dona de España* received that title because her travels started from Spain. A long, disastrous journey which created pandemic. She claimed more victims than the entire First World War.'

'Spanish flu.' The girl had spotted the reference at last. 'The outbreak of 1918. The death roll exceeded twenty million.'

'Twenty million at a conservative estimate, and the strain was not a normal flu virus. The Lady was a hybrid: that was what made her so lethal. Two separate organisms joined forces – her parents were *influentia coeli* and *vesiculla suis*. 'Yes, flu and swine fever, Jean. Commonplace illnesses that mated by chance and gave birth to a monster.' Mark was watching the drugged animal on the bench. Morphine had rendered it unconscious, but the disease remained active. The body was almost hairless now, and tumours were bulging out through the mottled skin. The results of a natural freak that had been resurrected and strengthened by human science.

'According to Mr Locke, Allan Carlin referred to his project as *La Dona*, so that's what the original element probably was.' Mark had turned and was looking at Jean Hedges. An attractive young woman. Almost as attractive as Tania, but neither would remain attractive when Carlin's Spanish Lady waved her wand at them.

Yes, very attractive. As attractive as another girl had been, if a photograph was any guide. Annabel Lee who would be about Tania's age if she was alive. A girl whom Edgar Godspel loved and another man wanted – Fred Brown who had carried the disease to Scotland.

'A brute, Sir Marcus.' Mark seemed to hear Mr Locke's actual voice. '. . . she found him repellent . . . he slapped her face . . . quite a scuffle till the doctor came on the scene . . . if ever a man had murder in his face . . .'

'Are you all right, sir?' Jean Hedges frowned, because Mark had closed his eyes for a moment. 'Shouldn't we be starting work?'

'Of course we should, and I'm perfectly well.' Mark moved to the bench and snapped the end off a plastic phial. Two theories, he thought, and his first notion appeared the most likely. At least he hoped it was. The second was far more sinister.

The Rushton Park research team had attempted to produce abnormally large domestic animals, and they had both succeeded and failed. Their creations were too large, too strong, and they were not domestic. They were wild beasts and also contagious. A demon had turned docile guinea-pigs into Gadarene swine. Uncontrollable monsters which had had to be destroyed. Was it possible that during their tussle in the laboratory Frederick Brown and Annabel Lee had also come into contact with that same demon?

Quite possible. They might have brushed against a cage, or overturned a culture saucer or broken a test tube and not known it. Mark opened another phial and mixed the two solutions to form a broth.

Frederick Brown must have been the first to experience the telltale symptoms and realize what had happened to him. Brown had hurried back to the laboratory and applied the antidote which was bound to have been available. Brown had halted the illness, but what would he have done then?

Mr Locke's statements and his association with James Clyde suggested that Brown was a vicious man. He would not have warned the girl who rejected and insulted him. He'd have poured the serum that could save her down a drain and burned the written formulae.

Brown had probably smiled when he heard that somebody else had visited the laboratory, and he'd known who that somebody was. Annabel Lee, seeking help and salvation and finding none. No serum, no information, no hope. A crazed, tormented creature who had ransacked the room and then staggered away to hide herself and die – helpless, alone, doomed.

But Fred Brown must have been hopeful. Mark looked at the two killers he had introduced to each other. Influenza and swine fever – the parents of a Spanish Lady. Yes, Frederick Brown believed that he'd killed the spores and was free of them. That the antidote was effective and he was out of danger.

Brown was wrong. The parasites had been rendered harmless and lain dormant in his system. They caused him no discomfort whatsoever, but they hadn't died. The spores were merely resting, and five years later radiation aroused them. During one morning or afternoon, one evening or night, on a remote Scottish peninsula, the Sleeping Beauties were awakened by Prince Charming's kiss.

What would Brown have done when he realized that the germ was active again and he was condemned to agony and mania? Who would his sick mind decide to punish? Mark tried to put himself in the man's position and it wasn't difficult. Annabel Lee was dead, nothing could harm her, but there was someone else who deserved to suffer. Fred Brown would have treated a piece of paper with blood, sputum or urine, and posted a letter to the person who had started it all – who was responsible for his malady.

To Dr Allan Carlin, the former inhabitant of Merrytor Cottage.

'Mrs Godspel is unavailable and I can tell you nothing.' Tania replaced the receiver. After the television announcement of Godspel's disappearance the phone had been constantly interrupting them. The public were eager for news, and so were the press. Five reporters had called at the door already, and through the window Tania could see two of them waiting in a parked car.

'Will they never stop – never leave me in peace?' Kathleen Godspel lay stretched out on the sofa, staring at the telephone like a rabbit hypnotized by a stoat.

'Before I knew that Edgar was dead, I kept willing that thing to ring, but now I can't stand any more, so please excuse me for a moment.' She heaved herself upright and walked to the door. Her hands dangled loosely from their wrists, and Tania saw that the knuckles were bruised. At some point, desperation had made the woman clench her fists and slam them against a wall or piece of furniture.

'We won't be disturbed any more, Tania. Not by the telephone that is, because I've taken off the bedroom extension.' Kate had returned and she stood beside the fireplace; her shoulders slumped and her head bowed. A sad, unattractive, ageing woman who had lost everything. 'Now, what were you asking me before those calls interrupted us?'

'Of course.' She straightened and lifted the photograph from the mantelshelf. 'You wanted to know about the Lady; the wicked Spanish Lady. La Española – the brain-child of my husband and his light of love; pretty little Annabel Lee.

'Yes, Edgar was involved in that Rushton business. One might almost say he was the prime mover.' She smiled at the face in the picture. 'Edgar was employed as a research biologist at Pertinax Productions when he first met Annabel and he'd been toying with the idea for some time. If plants can be stimulated by hormones and parasites – why not animals?

'A brilliant idea, but Edgar was a brilliant man in those days. Though he had no capital, Pertinax offered him a directorship. He turned it down after Annabel's death and drifted from job to job till he joined St Bede's. Guilt made my Edgar refuse that offer. If he'd accepted it, what do you imagine he'd be today?'

'Probably a millionaire.' Tania had no need to use her imagi-nation, because Pertinax Productions was the current Cinderella success-story. A small firm with a plant near Rushton that had specialized in agricultural germicides till excellent management and abnormal luck had changed the situation. Pertinax was now a giant – a vast financial empire controlling a dozen subsidiary companies.

'You say that Edgar took part in those experiments, Kate? That the original idea was his?' Tania realized the importance of the statements, but she couldn't concentrate. Something was interrupting her thoughts. Something which was probably quite innocent and she didn't know why it disturbed her. Workmen were digging a hole in a road. Children were kicking a football against a wall. A tug-boat was drawing a string of barges up the river.

'Edgar never actually took part in the experiments, Tania. He merely suggested the possibility to Annabel Lee and she talked it over with Carlin.' Kathleen Godspel replaced the photograph on its shelf. 'Carlin and Brown and Annabel did all the research work. Such a pity that they miscalculated and poor Annabel died.

'But what is the matter, my dear?' She had noted Tania's uneasiness. 'You are hardly listening to me.'

'I'm sorry, Kate.' The noise had stopped, but Tania was still disturbed. She was quite certain that it had not been caused by workmen or children or a motor engine. A faint, intermittent sound, but close to hand; or rather close to foot.

A sound which had appeared to come from under the floorboards, which was impossible. There was nothing under Kate Godspel's well-polished parquet floor; how could there be? Modern bungalows are rarely supplied with basements.

## Twenty-one

'Soon – very soon.' Mark's impatience was agonizing and his eyes kept darting from the laboratory clock to the surviving monkey which had been placed in a new cage before the morphine wore off. The animal's illness was still progressing in spite of his efforts to halt it; massive injections of Spanish flu serums.

'Yes, we'll know very soon, Jean, so do try and cheer up.' He forced himself to smile and appear confident. 'We're going to lick those little fiends, and while there's life there's hope.'

'There is also death, sir.' Though Jean Hedges had deep respect for Mark, she knew that his confidence was an act, and it didn't raise her spirits. Failure had depressed her professionally and she was also terrified for her own safety. What if the umbrella handle had been contaminated? What if the antiseptic had failed to kill the spores? In a short while she might be sharing the symptoms of that repellent, drugged creature behind the bars. 'None of the serums have had any effect at all.'

'I didn't really expect they would, Jean. We administered them too late.' Mark turned to the table and stared at a test tube which contained parts of himself. A blood sample which he had drawn from an artery and treated with a mixture of the vaccines. Mild heat had been applied to speed up the rate of infection and now it was time for the trial of strength.

'If that serum was in my system, I'd be running a temperature, but my antibodies, my protective devices, should have learned how to defend themselves.' He lifted a syringe and let a drop of the germ culture fall into the tube. 'Make up a slide, Jean, and we'll see how efficient their resistance is.'

Mark stepped away from the table and looked out of the laboratory window. St Bede's was a skyscraper block and the room was on the thirteenth floor. London lay spread out below him and somewhere among its myriad buildings Edgar Godspel might be found. Drunk or dead; suffering from amnesia, or suffering from disease.

The first and third possibilities were the most likely, Mark tried to reassure himself. The others were too bad to contemplate, and he thought of the questions he had put to Locke, and the replies which seemed to support his suppositions. Two suppositions and two sources of infection.

Annabel Lee who had hidden away to die: her body lying unnoticed for years, the spores dormant and inactive till someone touched the mummified flesh and the cycle was resumed.

Frederick Brown, who had applied the antidote and imagined he was safe. Who had lived without fear until radiation roused his sleeping parasites and he realized that he was condemned. Brown who had decided that Allan Carlin should share his agony.

Theories, suppositions and guesses, but there were actual facts to check at last. Jean Hedges had bent over a microscope and called him to join her.

'I wouldn't only be running a temperature, Jean, I'd be extremely ill.' Mark watched the battle raging on the slide, which he appeared to have lost. The alien units had rushed to the attack, and the human corpuscles were offering slight resistance. Cellular deformity was already apparent and his hopes were dashed.

Or were they? Almost in the exact centre of the picture there was a hint of retaliation. One of the blood cells had turned on its persecutors and others were following suit.

Yes, two – three – five, maybe twenty of them, were fighting

back and their numbers multiplied at every second. The invasion had taken the defenders by surprise, but they'd rallied and
a counter-attack was in progress. The whole slide showed that
the enemy were routed and on the run. White corpuscles with
induced immunity to the virus were more than a match for them
and Mark's hunch had paid off.

'You've done it, sir.' All Jean Hedges' fears had vanished and
her face was radiant. 'We've got an antidote – a cure and . . .
congratulations.'

'Mr Locke is the person to be congratulated, Jean. He has an
excellent memory.' Mark had seen enough and he straightened
from the microscope. Though victory was assured, he felt no pride
or sense of relief. He had not won a war, only a skirmish, and
success posed a question which was as disturbing as failure would
have been. He looked at the cage and frowned.

The animal was regaining consciousness and one of its eyes was
open and turned towards him. An eye full of hatred and malice
and he tried to imagine what other eyes had been like.

The eyes of somebody who had recovered from influenza
before the Rushton Park experiments were abandoned.

'We'll try to see that you're not bothered any more, madam, but
there's no sense in courting trouble.' The police sergeant had a
booming voice that reverberated around the bungalow. 'Why not
accept Lady Levin's invitation to go and stay at her house till the
scare dies down?'

'I intend to remain here.' Kate Godspel looked through the hall
window. Two uniformed constables were stationed outside the
front gate, and there was another in the back garden. The road was
clear of sightseers now, though it had been packed a few minutes
ago. Removing the telephone had given her and Tania no relief.
The public were as eager for information as the press and people
had arrived in shoals, ringing the doorbell and hammering on the
knocker. A fair-sized crowd had assembled before the police dis-
persed them.

'You are most considerate, officer, but I'm sure I shall be quite
all right.'

'I sincerely hope so, madam. We'll do the best we can.' The sergeant was about to leave, but he hesitated. 'And I suppose you haven't remembered anything that might help us regarding Dr Godspel's possible whereabouts. I don't want to be impertinent, but could he be with a girl-friend perhaps?'

'My husband was completely faithful to me, officer, and your question is impertinent . . . also unnecessary.' Tania saw Kathleen flush under her thick make-up. 'I promised your C.I.D. inspector that I'd contact him immediately if I recalled any valid facts and I will do so.'

'Of course, Mrs Godspel. Please accept my apologies.' He opened the door and glanced up and down the road. 'All quiet now, but people are inquisitive and morbid-minded and I'm afraid we can expect other would-be news hawks. My lads will keep them off the premises, but there may be the odd hooligan with a taste for stone-throwing. If you're determined to remain here, I'd advise drawing the curtains.'

'Stone-throwing!' The sergeant had left and Kate closed the door behind him. 'A man disappears and dies and the mob gather to hound his widow.

'What scum humanity is, Tania. Filthy, brainless, vicious humanity!' Her bruised hands clenched in anger, but that emotion was short-lived and she became pensive. 'I suppose one should expect such a response, though it's strange how curiosity and spite can sometimes be stronger than fear. People have been made to believe that Edgar is a danger to health, yet they come here to ask about him. To stand and gape in the hope of seeing him return.

'But that sergeant was right, my dear.' She lifted Tania's coat from a rack. 'There is a risk of violence and you mustn't share it. Though you've been very kind, I think you should leave now.'

'I want to stay if you'll let me.' Kathleen had held out the coat, but Tania shook her head. Curiosity could be stronger than fear, and stronger than pity. Though she was desperately sorry for Kate Godspel, she also wanted information.

'Of course I'd like you to stay.' Kate replaced the coat. 'Your company is just about one thing that's keeping me sane.' Tears were trickling from under her spectacles and she lowered her face.

'Sorry about that exhibition. Let's be practical and accept professional advice. If you'll draw the lounge curtains, I'll attend to the rest of the house, and then we'll have a nice cup of tea.'

Tea – Lee. The words rhymed. That was the only link between them, but they had set Tania's thoughts racing. She drew the curtains across the lounge window and switched on the lights. Wall lights and ceiling lights, and a brass miner's-lantern that stood beside the photograph above the fireplace and lit up the familiar face. She was positive that she had known that girl, and not merely seen her likeness in a newspaper or on a television screen. But how could she have done? She and Mark were in Russia when Annabel Lee was reported missing.

How – when – where had they met? By chance encounter at a cocktail- or dinner-party? In a restaurant or a theatre bar or during a journey? At one of the tedious scientific gatherings she sometimes attended for Mark's sake?

No, Tania was convinced that their relationship had been more intimate than that, though she couldn't concentrate. Sounds were interrupting her thoughts again. The kettle whistling in the kitchen, an airliner howling overhead, and the sound which had disturbed her before the doorbell started to ring. A dull, intermittent thudding noise which seemed to be coming from under the floorboards. Definitely coming from under the boards and Tania suspected a possible source. An unlikely suspicion, but if it was true she had reason to be alarmed.

Fate had played a very sick joke.

## Twenty-two

'That is quite definite. A person with recently developed immunity to any filter virus will recover from the illness, though serious and permanent damage occurs before it is checked.' Mark was telephoning Mr Roberts's secretary at the Ministry of Health. 'But Spanish flu vaccine provides complete protection. Both the spores and the organism are wiped out almost immediately and the patient experiences no adverse after-effects.'

Mark spoke with absolute confidence. The last monkey was dead. A lethal dose of morphine had given it peace before full consciousness returned, and smaller animals had told him the rest of the story. Leeches and sheep-ticks which he had inoculated against several strains of virus infection, and then subjected them to the germ culture.

Though all the creatures had survived, the majority had suffered changes which were apparent to the naked eye. Only the individuals protected by the Spanish flu serum were perfectly normal, and Mark's work was over. He had discovered an antidote and it was up to the authorities to do the rest.

'I understand that ample stocks of the vaccine are available, so you can act quickly. Set up immunization centres and see that everyone who could have been in contact with any of the victims gets a shot.

'I would also advise your Minister to issue a more truthful statement than his earlier one.' While they were waiting for the final results of their tests, Mark and Jean Hedges had heard Roberts's speech repeated on the radio.

'The Globe was irresponsible, but complacency can be as dangerous as panic. We have the means to prevent an epidemic provided people realize that the danger remains and inoculation is the sole safeguard.

'Goodbye.' Mark rang off abruptly, because two disturbing questions had entered his mind. A cure had been discovered and the enemy could be defeated if the defenders were prepared for the attack.

But how had the attack started, and who launched it? Not Frederick Brown as he had first imagined, and not Allan Carlin. They might have rendered themselves immune. They might have thrown off the effects of their illness, but it was unlikely. The signs of both inoculation and disease must have been apparent, and nobody had noticed them.

As he'd promised, Mr Locke had checked his files and delivered more information. The men had enjoyed good physical health during their stay at Rushton Park. Neither of them had lost a day through sickness or complained of any malaise.

Someone else had not been healthy, though. The third team member was less lucky. She had suffered from flu on two occasions. One bout at the beginning of the month – one on the day she vanished.

What had Annabel Lee looked like before her disappearance? Mark could only hazard a guess, but the creatures he had treated suggested the answer.

The leeches and the ticks were alive. They had come through their ordeal, though in different ways. A few were unblemished, but many were misshapen and riddled with tumours.

Deformities which had been halted before the terminal stages, and their significance set Mark's heart racing. Humanity could be provided with the necessary defences and he and Jean Hedges should be safe enough; the serum guaranteed that. But another person was not safe – not immune – and he had unknowingly persuaded her to risk infections.

'Oh, Tania,' Mark whispered, picking up the phone and dialling a number. 'Oh, my dear, lovely, Tania.'

'Yes, Tania, this bungalow was built on the foundations of an old Victorian house and the architect preserved the cellars as storage space.' Kathleen Godspel laid down a tea-tray on the table. 'But we've never used the basement, so how did you guess it existed?'

'Because there's something down there, Kate, and I heard it. Something or someone is moving about.' Though the noises had stopped, Tania was certain they would resume at any moment. 'You said that you kept searching the house for Edgar, but did you examine the basement?'

'There was no point. That is the only entrance to the cellars and it's locked.' She nodded at a heavy, panelled door behind Tania's back. 'It has always been locked and what you heard were commonplace noises. Traffic and aircraft and boats on the river.

'You have a vivid imagination, Tania, and I appreciate your anxiety. Edgar must have been infected while he was helping Mark and he would have tried to kill himself. Edgar knew what the Lady can do – who knew better?

'But you believe that he came home, took an overdose of sleeping pills and went down into the cellars to die. That the suicide attempt failed and he recovered. That he is stumbling about in the dark . . . drugged, diseased, scarcely human.

'An unnerving prospect, but I can assure you that you're wrong. Drugs are unreliable, and if Edgar had decided to return here and kill himself, he would have used one of those – one of his toys.' Kate pointed at the collection of guns on the walls. 'And even if Edgar had taken pills and locked himself in the cellars, how do you account for this?' She opened the drawer of a desk. 'The only key to the door and here it is. Are you satisfied at last?'

'No, because I'm sure there is someone down there, Kate.' Though the key was held out for her inspection, Tania was unconvinced. The sounds had been real. She had heard them as distinctly as she could hear the clock ticking away beside the miner's-lamp and the picture of Annabel Lee.

'Listen – just listen!' She swung round. Other noises had started. No intermittent thuds, but footsteps. Heavy, steady, purposeful footsteps mounting a staircase. 'Are you deaf or trying to deceive yourself, Kate?'

'Neither, my dear. I'm merely surprised, because the possibility never occurred to me.' The key had dropped from Kathleen Godspel's hand and she gripped the desk to support herself. 'How could Edgar have broken through that wall? Annabel used quick-setting cement.'

'The police.' Tania had not realized the significance of the last statement. The footsteps had ceased and other sounds were replacing them. Sobbing, grunting sounds and the crashes of fists hammering against woodwork. 'We must get out of here and tell the police, Kate.'

'Stay where you are.' Tania had started to hurry towards the hall, but Kathleen Godspel clutched her shoulder. Though the cellar door was shaking, she had regained her composure and spoke quite calmly.

'The police are unarmed. Why should they risk their lives when Edgar is my responsibility?

'My entire responsibility, Tania.' She released her grip and lifted

an automatic pistol from the drawer. 'This is Edgar's only modern weapon. A silenced Luger which he always keeps loaded. How
naughty of him! How illegal! How fitting that a treasured posses-
sion should be his executioner.'

'Don't, Kate . . . don't shoot. Edgar is ill, but he's still a human
being. Your husband . . . a man who loved you.' It was Tania's turn
to clutch out, but Kathleen's free arm swung at her like a flail and
she reeled sideways.

'Did he love me – really love me?' The pistol was aimed at the
door and the woman's hand tightened on the trigger. 'Maybe he
did once – long ago. But love flew away and all he felt was guilt and
remorse and pity.

'The only girl Edgar loved was Annabel Lee and they destroyed
each other. Edgar ruined little Annie . . . he corrupted her, body,
soul and mind, and that's why . . .'

The sentence went unfinished, because there was no time for
speech. The door was being forced away from its lock and hinges.
A panel had disintegrated to reveal the lion-faced thing from the
cellar and Tania's compassion turned to loathing.

'Kill him, Kate,' she shouted, and then changed the pronoun.
'Kill *It* – kill *It* – kill *It*.'

## Twenty-three

'An antidote is available . . . supplies of the serum are in stock
. . . Immunization centres are being set up . . . there is no cause for
alarm.' The promises rasped reassuringly from a loudspeaker van,
but Mark cursed the man delivering them. A driver who hugged
the crown of the narrow, suburban road and was quite oblivious
to the blasts of his horn.

'Locations of the centres will be issued in due course, but in the
meantime, we must keep calm. The epidemic has been contained,
and the risk to health is negligible.'

*Available – contained – no cause for alarm – negligible.* Half-truths
and lies, Mark thought. The vaccine did give immunity provided
it was administered before infection. A person who had recently

suffered from conventional flu would throw off the illness, though its scars would remain. But without such defences, there was no hope – none at all. The patient would be condemned to agony, deformity and mania.

'Get out of my way, damn you.' Mark cursed the driver holding him back. He cursed the telephone-operator who had told him that the Godspels' number was out of order. He cursed himself – most of all he cursed himself – and what a fool he was!

He should have guessed why Edgar Godspel had muttered that excuse and left the laboratory. Edgar had not been ill or drunk or infected. He hadn't hidden away to die, as Annabel Lee was said to have done. The man's motivation could have been quite logical.

'Thank God!' The van had finally edged towards the kerb and Mark stamped on the accelerator. 'Also, please God,' he thought, 'Please let me get there soon . . . please show me that I'm wrong about Edgar . . . please may Tania have left.' His eyes glanced at the speedometer and the dashboard clock. Pace and time – the two enemies.

He was driving far faster than the safety limit, but it was almost an hour since he had left the hospital. In spite of Mr Roberts's broadcast, public unrest was mounting. Westminster had been thronged with anxious crowds and irate demonstrators, and Trafalgar Square was impassable. Mark had had to make long side-street detours to escape the traffic jams.

But he was nearing journey's end at last. There was the river – there was the block of flats Kathleen Godspel had complained of before Lawrence telephoned and his involvement began – there was the turn off. Tyres screamed as Mark took the bend and then he slammed on his brakes to avoid the parked cars and the groups of sightseers. The road to Godspel's bungalow was blocked by a cordon and a barrier.

A similar barrier to those with which Jaimie Clyde had closed the roads to Ben Sagur.

'The beast is dead, Tania, and that, I think, is that.' Kathleen Godspel had fired five shots before lowering the pistol and her victim looked dead enough. He looked as though he had never been alive

– never human. Certainly he bore no resemblance to Edgar Godspel, the little doctor of science who collected jokes and weapons.
The body was far larger than a normal man's and the bullets had
swung it sideways when the door burst open. It lay stretched out
across the shattered timbers; face upright and eyes open.

'Yes, that's my Edgar, Tania. Don't you recognize his suit and
his old school tie and his silly Rotary Club pin?' Kathleen pointed
at her husband, and Tania did recognize the clothes, though there
wasn't much left of them. Fragments of cloth smeared with dust
and cement and plaster and blood. Rags with the seams ripped
apart by the swelling, fungoid-like flesh.

'Don't look so shocked, Tania; so disapproving. I had to kill
him.' The woman placed the automatic beside the tea-tray. 'There
was no other choice and you told me to. "Kill it," you said. "Kill
it – kill it – kill it." '

'Yes, I did say that.' Though Tania was still half-stunned, she
remembered other words that had been said when the footsteps
started to mount the stairs. Words spoken in astonishment. 'Annabel used quick-setting cement.' She and Kathleen were not alone.
There was a third person in the house.

'Of course you had to kill him, Kate. No one would have wanted
Edgar to go on living.' Tania looked away from the hideous figure
on the door and studied the photograph above the fireplace. She
knew where she had met the girl at last. She knew almost everything, but she had to keep her head. She had to put on a convincing
act of ignorance. 'There is no reason for you to reproach yourself,
Kate; none at all.'

'You are very understanding, my dear. Also very brave, though
I'm sure you could do with a pick-me-up.' Kathleen's hand hovered
over the tray. 'But how bad my memory is. I've quite forgotten
whether you take milk and sugar.'

'Neither, Kate. Only plain tea because I'm on a slimming diet.'
Tania turned from the picture and watched her hostess fill a cup.
Though it seemed like hours since she heard the kettle whistle, the
pot had an insulated cover and the tea was still steaming.

'Thank you, Kate. A pick-me-up, as you said, and just what I
need.' Tania stepped forward and took the cup from her. 'What we

all need, Kate: the three of us; you and I and Annabel.'

She reached out, snatched off the woman's glasses and threw the hot liquid into her face.

'Everybody wants to visit that bungalow, sir. To stand and gawp, pester Mrs Godspel and create disturbances.' Mark had wound down the car window and made his request, but the police sergeant was adamant. 'That's why we've closed the road and it's going to stay closed till people come to their senses.' He scowled at the sightseers gathered before the barrier. 'Only residents and persons on urgent business are being allowed through, so why should you be treated as an exception?'

'Because my business is urgent, and . . .' Mark reached for a visiting-card in his wallet, because speech was useless and another loudhailer van was drowning his words with orders and encouragements.

'Please disperse and return to your homes and places of employment. There is no cause for alarm or panic. Vaccine is already being distributed to all local authorities and the Minister of Health has just made a further statement.

'Mr Roberts is confident that . . .'

'Sir Marcus Levin, eh?' The statement had ended at last and Mark's card impressed the policeman. 'K.C.B., eh? Fellow of the Royal Society, eh?

'Yes, I've heard of you, sir. I'll go and have a word with my inspector. I've also had the pleasure of meeting your wife who is keeping Mrs Godspel company. A very charming young lady if I may say so.'

'You can say what you like, but there's no time to talk to anybody. You must allow me to pass.' Tania was still in the bungalow. One of Mark's prayers had gone unanswered and he was about to sound his horn, force a way through the crowd and ram the road block. An unnecessary action, because a constable with a two-way radio had hurried over to deliver a message.

'Let us through, lads.' The sergeant shouted at the men manning the barrier and climbed into the back of the car. 'Get going sir,' he said, and not because Mark's credentials were impressive.

He had three assistants stationed outside the bungalow and they had all heard a woman scream.

## Twenty-four

'A good try, very good, though it was bound to fail. Two individuals are usually a match for one.' The voice was very close to her and Tania's memory was returning. After throwing the cup she had run into the hall and reached the front door. But before she could open the door something slammed against the back of her head and darkness came.

'I'm sorry Annabel had to hit you with the pistol, but we're sure there's no fracture and you'll soon be your old self again.'

'Your old self – what a stupid remark to make.' The words were interrupted by a cackle of laughter. 'You're young, my sweet. Just about our own age, and as lovely as we used to be. Open your eyes and see what we look like now.'

'I know what you look like and I know who you are.' Tania's eyelids remained tightly closed. 'But I don't know why . . . what made you do it.'

'Not an easy question to answer. I suppose something just came over us, as they say.' There was another mocking laugh. 'Or was fate involved? Nemesis?

'Yes, Nemesis must have guided Kathleen to that copy of *Life and History*, Tania. The doctor had just confirmed that her brain tumour was malignant and she was so wretched and frightened. All she could look forward to was insanity and death, and life had no purpose. Then she opened the magazine, saw Frederick Brown's picture staring out at her, and there was a purpose again; a job to be done.

'Brown was alive and he had to be punished. God ordered Kate and Annabel to punish him. Wise God – wicked Fred Brown.

'Fred Brown lost his temper in the laboratory and attacked poor Annabel. He threw her against a rack of test tubes, and one of the tubes was unstoppered. Brown had to suffer and so had Carlin.' The accents kept varying from sentence to sentence and

Tania was uncertain how many people were speaking.

'Stupid, incompetent, old Carlin. He was fascinated when I told him about Edgar's idea of creating superior animals, and he never considered the dangers. Carlin miscalculated and what were the results?

'Uncontrollable freaks that had to be destroyed. Monsters which we have resurrected because Annabel was foresighted and she thought of the future. After she went back to the lab and burned the records, she removed a sample of the culture and we preserved it for five whole years.

'Were you foresighted or merely impulsive, Annie?' The speaker sounded genuinely puzzled. 'We'll never be sure, Tania, because it happened so long ago and Annie was sick. She was ill and bewildered and she can't really remember her feelings. If she hadn't had flu before that devil pushed her against the rack – if Edgar hadn't nursed her, she might have died. How fortunate that would have been for you, my dear.

'Poor, silly, sentimental Edgar. No, clever, treacherous Edgar.' The words were literally spat out and saliva sprayed Tania's chin. 'While he was at the hospital with Mark, Edgar suspected that the Spanish Lady was on the move again. That's why he hurried back here and accused us . . . why he had to join Brown and Carlin.'

'So you infected him.' Tania tried to get up, but realized it was impossible. She had been stretched out on the sofa and her wrists and ankles were tied to its legs. 'You poisoned Edgar and walled him up in a cellar to die in agony. Your own husband . . . the man who nursed you and married you in spite . . .'

'In spite of what?' A hand – one of the bruised hands that had beaten Edgar Godspel unconscious – slapped Tania's cheek. 'You've never seen the women Edgar married, so do as I said. Open your eyes and have a good look at us.'

'I am looking.' Tania obeyed at last, but she didn't scream. Not immediately, though what she saw was disturbing. Two faces were posed above her and despite the extreme changes it was clear that they had a single owner. The face of a girl who would have been pretty if her expression wasn't so hard and intelligent. A young, lifeless face on a photograph, and a living, scarred, prematurely-aged face.

'That's right, my dear. Have a good, long look, though you haven't seen anything yet.' Mrs Godspel – the once lovely Annabel Lee – raised a hand and Tania did scream. She screamed because the woman was removing her hair.

The long, dark glistening hair which was her sole physical attraction. False hair that came away from her head. A wig to hide the horror behind it.

'Don't open that door.' Mark jumped out of the car and dashed down the path to the bungalow with the sergeant at his heels. One of the constables had broken a glass panel with his truncheon and was groping for the lock. 'Nobody must go inside . . . no one except myself.'

Mark was certain that it was Tania who had screamed, but though he needed help he couldn't expose others to infection. His left armpit was throbbing painfully, the serum had taken effect, but the policemen had no such protection.

'The house may be a death-trap, so stay where you are.' He released the catch and then nodded at the man's truncheon. As poor a weapon as the umbrella which had stunned the monkey, but all that was available. 'I'm going in alone and you can lend me that.'

'Thank you.' The man handed him the short, heavy stick and he opened the door and walked forward.

'Come in . . . Come in, whoever you are.' His entry had been heard and a voice jibbered the parody of a song as he crossed the hall. A cracked, insane voice which told him the worst. 'All the gang's here, so hurry along and join the fun and games. The more the merrier, sergeant, or constable or whatever your rank is.

'You – you, Sir Marcus. The very last person we expected, but how glad we are to welcome you.' The woman standing beside the sofa shook with laughter. 'Not a policeman, but the hero of the hour; the great man himself. The world-famous bacteriologist who has defeated *the Lady* – The lovely Spanish Lady, if that loud-speaker message is true.'

'The statement was correct.' Mark had stopped in the doorway
of the sitting room with the truncheon dangling uselessly from his
hand, and he felt helpless and terrified. Tania was tied to the sofa,
and Edgar Godspel – what had once been Edgar Godspel – lay
across another broken door; dead and deformed and hideous.

But it wasn't Edgar's appearance that frightened Mark. Nor
did the woman who had greeted him, though she was almost as
repellent. The deep scars and wrinkles surrounding the eyes, the
hairless skull furrowed by the pustules that had tortured her till
resistance to influenza halted their growth.

'Then we must congratulate you, mustn't we?' She laughed
again and Mark realized that he was at odds with the ultimate
form of schizophrenia; mental and physical. Two individuals sharing a sick mind and a sick body. The girl Edgar Godspel loved and
the woman he had married.

An unnerving phenomenon, but not the most alarming one. An
inanimate object kept Mark motionless in the doorway. A hypodermic syringe was poised over Tania's arm.

'Our heartiest congratulations, Sir Marcus. You have been as
brilliant as usual, but what a shame that you discovered the antidote too late to save your pretty Tania.' Her thumb was steady
on the syringe plunger. 'Tania will soon resemble me; or rather,
resemble him.' The woman nodded at Godspel, but she didn't look
round. She was enjoying her revenge and Mark's expression produced another crackle of laughter.

'Why do you want to injure Tania, Mrs Godspel?' Though
he thought he knew all the answers Mark had to play for time,
because there was hope . . . there was a weapon.

Not the truncheon, and not the pistol on the table. They were
useless, and the injection would be made before the stick was
raised or the gun pointed and fired. Mark's hopes were centred on
an ally – a human being. 'What harm has Tania ever done you?'

'Tania tried to blind me, Sir Marcus. She threw a cup of hot tea
in my eyes, though I suppose we can't blame her for that, can we,
Annabel?' There was a hint of puzzlement on the scarred face.
'No, I'm not really sure what our exact reasons are.'

'You have several reasons and they are all understandable.' Mark was still playing for time and he willed Tania not to speak or move, because someone else was moving. Someone who had not died was starting to crawl across the floor; wounded, monstrous and in agony; also sad. Though the eyeballs were red and swollen out of all natural proportions, Mark could see the misery behind them.

'Tania may have tried to blind you, but that's only one of your motives for hurting her. She happens to be very beautiful and you envy her, Kate. You hate her because she is beautiful, Annabel Lee.'

'How right you are, Sir Marcus, but then you're always right. Clever, fortunate Marcus Levin, the lucky Polish Jew.' The hypodermic needle moved closer to Tania's arm. 'Though you won't be so fortunate much longer. Not where marriage is concerned. Your wife is going to lose her looks and I'll tell you why . . . what the real reason is. I've just remembered why I want to destroy Tania. I know who is really to blame.'

'Don't – don't – please don't.' Time was up, the needle was about to enter a vein and Mark sprang forward, the truncheon swinging in his right hand and his left fist clenched.

An intervention which came too late and was unnecessary. Other hands saved Tania Levin.

# Postscript

'1968; the July issue. Thanks, Bill. Thank you for telling me.' Mark laid down the telephone. 'Thank you very much indeed. As usual you are a fund of information.'

'What is the matter, darling?' Mark had spoken to himself after ringing off and Tania sensed his tension. 'The vaccine does work. They've proved it's a hundred per cent effective, so why are you worried?' A week had passed and Tania's confidence appeared justifiable. No further cases of the illness had been reported and the serum did provide complete immunity. 'What are you looking for?'

'For proof of guilt.' They were in the library and Mark crossed to a section of technical books. 'I've just remembered something significant, or rather been reminded of it.'

Memory is an adaptable gift, he thought while his eyes ran along the shelves. The brain dismisses certain experiences because they are too intolerable to bear. One of his own experiences was a typical example.

Mark could still see Edgar Godspel's hands dragging Kate away from Tania, and still hear the crack as he broke Kate's neck. He could still hear the grunting, piglike sounds Godspel had made when he staggered up from the floor and lurched towards the sofa. He could still feel the recoils of the automatic pistol as he pressed the trigger and its remaining bullets sent Godspel's hideous body reeling back across the woman he once loved, but had had to kill. The spreader of disease, who had posted those tainted letters to Brown and Carlin. Annabel Lee, who'd infected her own husband and hoped to destroy others; many, many others.

Though the Godspels were dead and at rest now, their images would haunt Mark for some time and then become vague and shadowy. An early memory had returned to trouble him.

'There's nothing the matter, Tania; nothing to worry about. The Spanish Lady has ended her journey and we can smile again.' Mark tried to smile, but the attempt was as false as Sir James Fraser Clyde's last smile and he realized why the Smilin' Boy had asked him to be present during that appeal for help. Jaimie Clyde had known that radiation was not involved and he'd begun to suspect the truth. An unpleasant truth, but it must be faced, and Mark also realized why Kate Godspel had hated Tania and himself.

'A project at Rushton Park worked too well,' he said. 'The research team created demons and five years later those demons were resurrected and over two hundred people died.' Mark lifted a book from one of the shelves. 'Not a severe death roll. A minor tragedy, but who was responsible? Who caused it all?

'Edgar Godspel, who suggested the idea to Annabel Lee? Dr Carlin, who ignored the risks and miscalculated? Fred Brown, who lost his temper when a girl rejected him? Kate Godspel, who developed a brain tumour and went crazy?' Mark had checked the book's index and found the reference he wanted. 'No, they were only pawns, so who was the prime mover? Who is really to blame?

'That was Bill Lawrence on the phone and he told me that the police found copies of this in Brown's lodgings, Carlin's cottage and the Godspels' bungalow. In each instance the title was underlined and there were pencilled notes in the margins.' He handed the volume to Tania. Bound issues of an obscure medical journal open at an article he had forgotten till Lawrence called. A thesis abandoned long ago. *Viral Mutation and the Inducement of Giantism.*

'Who is really to blame?' Mark repeated. 'Who was the originator – the true culprit?' He pointed to the author's name at the foot of the page and nodded.

'Yes, Tania,' he said. 'I am.'

# ALSO AVAILABLE FROM VALANCOURT BOOKS

| | |
|---|---|
| Michael Arlen | Hell! said the Duchess |
| R. C. Ashby (Ruby Ferguson) | He Arrived at Dusk |
| Frank Baker | The Birds |
| Walter Baxter | Look Down in Mercy |
| Charles Beaumont | The Hunger and Other Stories |
| David Benedictus | The Fourth of June |
| Paul Binding | Harmonica's Bridegroom |
| Charles Birkin | The Smell of Evil |
| John Blackburn | A Scent of New-Mown Hay |
| | Broken Boy |
| | Blue Octavo |
| | A Ring of Roses |
| | The Flame and the Wind |
| | Nothing but the Night |
| | Bury Him Darkly |
| | The Household Traitors |
| | Our Lady of Pain |
| | Devil Daddy |
| | The Face of the Lion |
| | The Cyclops Goblet |
| | A Beastly Business |
| | The Bad Penny |
| Thomas Blackburn | A Clip of Steel |
| | The Feast of the Wolf |
| John Braine | Room at the Top |
| | The Vodi |
| Jack Cady | The Well |
| Michael Campbell | Lord Dismiss Us |
| R. Chetwynd-Hayes | The Monster Club |
| Basil Copper | The Great White Space |
| | Necropolis |
| Hunter Davies | Body Charge |
| Jennifer Dawson | The Ha-Ha |
| Barry England | Figures in a Landscape |
| Ronald Fraser | Flower Phantoms |
| Gillian Freeman | The Liberty Man |
| | The Leather Boys |
| | The Leader |

| | |
|---|---|
| J.B. PRIESTLEY | The Magicians |
| | Saturn Over the Water |
| | The Thirty-First of June |
| | The Shapes of Sleep |
| | Salt Is Leaving |
| PETER PRINCE | Play Things |
| PIERS PAUL READ | Monk Dawson |
| FORREST REID | Following Darkness |
| | The Spring Song |
| | Brian Westby |
| | The Tom Barber Trilogy |
| | Denis Bracknel |
| GEORGE SIMS | Sleep No More |
| | The Last Best Friend |
| ANDREW SINCLAIR | The Facts in the Case of E. A. Poe |
| | The Raker |
| COLIN SPENCER | Panic |
| DAVID STOREY | Radcliffe |
| | Pasmore |
| | Saville |
| MICHAEL TALBOT | The Delicate Dependency |
| RUSSELL THORNDIKE | The Slype |
| | The Master of the Macabre |
| JOHN TREVENA | Sleeping Waters |
| JOHN WAIN | Hurry on Down |
| | The Smaller Sky |
| | Strike the Father Dead |
| | A Winter in the Hills |
| KEITH WATERHOUSE | There is a Happy Land |
| | Billy Liar |
| COLIN WILSON | Ritual in the Dark |
| | Man Without a Shadow |
| | The World of Violence |
| | The Philosopher's Stone |
| | The God of the Labyrinth |

FOR MORE INFORMATION AND A COMPLETE LIST OF TITLES, PLEASE VISIT
OUR WEBSITE AT WWW.VALANCOURTBOOKS.COM

CPSIA information can be obtained
at www.ICGtesting.com
Printed in the USA
BVHW08215418102
649669BV00004B/195

9 781939 140432